A GILDED AGE CHRISTMAS

Amanda McCabe
and
Lauri Robinson

MILLS & BOON

A GILDED AGE CHRISTMAS

Amanda McCabe
and
Lauri Robinson

MILLS & BOON

First published in Great Britain 2023
by Mills & Boon, an imprint of HarperCollins*Publishers* Ltd,
1 London Bridge Street, London, SE1 9GF

www.harpercollins.co.uk

HarperCollins*Publishers*, Macken House, 39/40 Mayor Street Upper,
Dublin 1, D01 C9W8, Ireland

A Gilded Age Christmas
© 2023 Harlequin Enterprises ULC

A Convenient Winter Wedding © 2023 Amanda McCabe
The Railroad Baron's Mistletoe Bride © 2023 Lauri Robinson

ISBN: 978-0-263-30542-5

10/23

This book is produced from independently certified FSC™ paper to ensure responsible forest management.
For more information visit: www.harpercollins.co.uk/green.

Printed and Bound in the UK using 100% Renewable Electricity at CPI Group (UK) Ltd, Croydon, CR0 4YY

CONTENTS

A CONVENIENT
WINTER WEDDING

Amanda McCabe

Prologue

Newport, summer 1882

May Van Der Berg absolutely, positively, completely wished she was anywhere else.

She went up on tiptoe to peer through the window at the ballroom, aching with the hope that no one would see her, that she could linger there in the garden just a little longer. She knew it was terribly rude to the hostess—her godmother and her mother's best friend, Mrs. Gorley—but she was so sure she was about to suffocate under all that gilt and marble and satin, and she wanted to breathe.

As much as she *could* breathe in her new silk-and-tulle confection from Madame Osborne's atelier, that was. She plucked at the tight bodice, all pleated tucks and bows, so perfect for a young lady in her first season "out." So wonderfully tasteful and stylish, but not *too* stylish. Van Der Bergs were never too stylish. They had been in New York since they'd arrived from the town of Berg en Dal in Holland in the 1650s; they had no need for Paris gowns straight out of the box, for Doucet and Worth. Tulle frocks from Madame Osborne and discreet pearl necklaces were the correct thing, and Van Der Bergs were always and completely *correct*.

Correct—and too expensive. Even May knew that, though her parents tried so hard to hide such matters from her, to hide her father's poor investments. The missing paintings on the walls of their Washington Square brownstone; the decrease in horses and silver and dinner parties. The dry chicken and boiled vegetables on their table. How ridiculous to spend money on frocks now, especially ones she disliked wearing! Or to spend money on a summer in Newport, just because that was where they always went.

Not that Newport had been all terrible. It never was. May loved the sea, the salty coolness of it on her skin as she swam at Bailey's Beach. The clear air and sunshine, lawn tennis and drives and tea parties. And it helped that Van Der Bergs did not stay in grand cottages along Ochre Point. Even if they could have afforded such a place—which they definitely could not. May's grandmother had a place beyond Spring Street, farther inland, where the shore gave way to scrubby moors and fields. A lovely, faded shingled old house, with rambling rooms and large lawns for games. She'd always enjoyed it there, but this summer was different. This summer she was officially a grown lady, and the future had crashed down on her.

She'd been brought "out" in the winter. A tea and musicale at her grandmother's house a few doors down from her parents', where all their old friends had gathered. Van Der Bergs, and Skuytercliffs such as her mother had been, just as they didn't shop at Worth or have great marble summer cottages, didn't have lobster suppers and balls at Delmonico's. Which May thought was a pity, as that all sounded very fun, and she did enjoy good suppers, which her mother and grandmother cared nothing about. Lobster and canvasback duck would be so nice after so much broiled shad.

The guests at that tea had been people she'd always known, of course, Fishes and Van Rensselaers and Livingstons, and one of her oldest friends, Ellen Driver. There were young men she'd once danced with at Dodsworth's Dancing Academy, had run with on the beach at Newport and gone sledding with in Central Park. Boys she'd always known. But now there was such a different feeling around it all. A tension, an awkwardness. Her old friends didn't visit so much now that everyone knew her father's fortune was diminished, and her suitors had vanished. Not that they were so terrific in the first place. She only wanted to marry for real affection, real love.

But, oh, it could be a bit lonely!

And she did know, even though her parents never said such things aloud, that she had to get married soon, and not just any marriage. One with a fine income attached, a security. So this summer was not all croquet on her grandmother's ramshackle lawn and swimming in the sea with friends. This summer, May's mother and Mrs. Gorley—her mother's one true and loyal friend, who had the good fortune to marry a very wealthy man indeed and was now one of the leaders of society, who *did* have cottages and Worth gowns and diamond tiaras—had taken her to dressmaker after dressmaker, trying to "make the best" of her face and figure. Had given her lessons in entertaining and French and music, beyond what she'd learned all her life. Taught her how to smile and walk and laugh.

It all culminated in this ball.

May sighed as she watched the dancers spinning and twirling on the glass-bright parquet floor under the glow of dripping-waterfall-style chandeliers, their amethyst and cream and candy-pink and emerald-green gowns and flashing diamonds crackling and shifting like a kaleidoscope, set against the stark black and white of the men's evening suits. She glimpsed Mrs. Gorley through the crowd, her godmother's tall, stately figure draped in amber-gold taffeta fastened with her famous diamond stomacher, her dark hair swept high and held with a topaz bandeau. She was obviously searching for someone, her feather fan sweeping in agitated fashion. May was sure she was looking for *her*.

May did love her parents dearly, and Mrs. Gorley, too. They'd done everything for her, their only child. The best governesses, dancing classes, music lessons, travel, friends. And she knew she owed them a fine marriage, owed them the satisfaction and peace of mind of seeing her well settled, the comfort of their later age.

But why, why did it have to be like *this*? She wanted to care about someone she had to spend her life with, and longed for someone to care about her. To *see* her, the real her. Someone she could be herself with for years to come.

She tried not to be romantic, she really did. There was so little room for the frivolity of *romance* in the Van Der Bergs' ordered and sensible world. Yet the books she read in secret, French and Italian romances about gallant knights and fair maidens and danger and adventure, made her wish so much that there might be more in the world. Might be passion, and color, and—yes, and love.

Those dreams shattered as she glimpsed her mother moving across the ballroom to meet Mrs. Gorley. Adeline Van Der Berg looked much like May, small and slim and fair-skinned, but her delicacy was deceptive. She had a will of iron; she had to in New York society, despite her old name. She smiled gently as she walked, her dove-gray satin gown shimmering, but she did not look happy she couldn't find May.

May ducked down, dropping her ruffled train and snatching it back up again before it trailed in the mud of the azalea beds. She'd get enough of a scolding for missing both the mazurka and the first quadrille; she didn't need a ruined gown, too.

Yet neither could she quite make herself go back inside just yet. She dashed away from the house, hoping no one saw her.

As she ran down the manicured lawn that sloped toward the dark sea, the music and chatter of the ball faded, and the quiet of the night softly started to close around her. She heard the call of a bird out over the water, the burble of the fountains Mrs. Gorley had scattered through her gardens.

She found the small teahouse at the edge of the lawn, and paused there to catch her breath. Madame Osborne's gowns, appropriate as they might be, weren't quite made for mad dashes into too-brief freedom. She gazed back at the house, awash in moonlight.

She had to admit, her godmother certainly knew how to throw a party, a skill she'd tried for years to impart to May. The veranda was laid with small round tables, draped in pale pink damask and lit with strings of paper lanterns that cast a rosy glow over everything. More lanterns led the way along the garden paths, and candles floated in the fountains. The house itself was lit up like a giant chandelier.

May had to confess she would rather like that part of having some money. To entertain and bring enjoyment to people; to work for charities as she chose; to meet whom she wanted and have parties as she planned them. If only she didn't have to marry to achieve it!

And marry whom? That was the real conundrum.

She glanced back over her shoulder at the sea. The tiny flickering lights of boats moored there blinked in the night. She knew a few of them, had sailed in some, but there was one that was new. And far grander than all the rest. Two hundred and eighty feet, she would estimate, three-masted, gleaming white.

"If only I could turn pirate and steal *that* vessel," she murmured. "I'd sail and sail and sail, and never come back."

"I could arrange that," said a voice, deep and rich, touched with a slight, lilting accent. "No piracy necessary. I think it would be hard to sail such a vessel all by yourself, in that gown."

She was not alone.

May's heart seemed to shudder under the satin bows of her unsuitable for sailing gown, and then pounded even harder. She felt icy cold and burning with embarrassment all at the same time.

She whirled around and saw the tiny red glowing end of a cigarillo in the shadows of the little teahouse, with the silhouette of a man seated on the iron chaise behind it. A very tall, broad-shouldered man.

"I beg your pardon," she stammered. "I didn't mean to intrude."

"You're not. Indeed, this is the most interesting thing to happen all evening." He rose slowly, gracefully, to his feet, one smooth movement like an expert dancer or—no, like a jungle cat. A panther, lazy, indolent, a long, rippling stretch just before pouncing. He stepped into the golden glow of the lanterns, and May gasped.

She'd never seen him before. She was utterly sure of that, as she would have remembered. He wasn't like most of the men she met at parties, men who talked of sports and their clubs and spun her somewhat awkwardly on the dance floor as she was meant to beam up at them in rapt fascination. This man was tall, much taller than her own sadly petite stature, and lean in a way that only horseback riding and trekking over moors, or even more strenuous exercise, could give a man.

He was perfectly, impeccably dressed, his black suit obviously from Brooks Brothers, sparkling white shirt from Kaskel and Kaskel, cream waistcoat gleaming, matched perfectly by the white carnation in his buttonhole. So she knew he was a guest, but her godmother hadn't presented him to her. And, though he fit in with all the other people in the ballroom, their dark suits and flowers and gleaming patent shoes, he also didn't fit in at all.

He had dark hair, so dark and lustrous it seemed part of the night, and it was a bit longer than it should be, one wave even falling over his brow. He impatiently flicked it back, revealing a face meant to be carved in Italian friezes, painted in murals on villa walls. A Medici or Borgia or something like that. High, sharply carved cheekbones, slanting dark brows, full, enticingly soft-looking lips above a square jaw. And his nose—well, his nose should have been a perfect blade, as befit a Renaissance prince, but it had clearly been broken and healed awkwardly at one time. Strangely, it just made him even more handsome.

May realized she'd been staring, gawking even, against every bit of her careful training in manners, and she stepped back and lowered her eyes. Maybe if she quit looking directly at him, she wouldn't be so dazzled. He was like sunlight on the summer sea. Then she realized she could *smell* him, a delicious, lightly spicy scent of his soap and clean, crisp linen.

Well, she couldn't just stand there like a ninny-hammer. She couldn't quite bring herself to leave, either. She thought of all those novels she'd devoured in secret, tales of adventure and passion and dashing men, and how she'd always thought she could never meet someone like that. This man, whoever he was, seemed to have more potential than anyone she'd ever met before.

She turned back to look at the yacht at its moorings, and heard the crisp rustle of fine wool and linen as he put out the cigarillo in a tall silver ashtray and took a step closer to her. "Are you contemplating an escape, too?" she asked.

"Just a quiet moment. Mrs. Gorley's invitations are too sought-after to just ditch." He leaned against the iron frame of the doorway, and she sensed him cross his arms over his chest as he watched her. Studied her, as she had studied him. "I might make an escape with the right company, though. Moonlight on the waves, champagne on deck…"

May laughed. Not the soft, ladylike giggle her mother approved at the appropriate moments, but a full, startled guffaw. She pressed her gloved fingertips to her lips and shook her head. It was the tiniest of light flirtations he offered, though even a few words in that deep, accented voice of his took on darker meanings. No one had ever spoken quite like that to May Van Der Berg, either, suggesting a moonlight sail with champagne, all alone! Shocking.

And what delightful images it brought. A wave of desire, carried on salt waves and wine, this man's body pressed close to hers...

"There is moonlight here," she said. "And champagne. Well—no champagne *right* here, but in the ballroom. Which we have escaped."

"So we have. And—ah! What have we here?" He leaned over and drew an open bottle from behind one of the iron chairs.

May laughed again. "Are you a wizard, then, sir?"

"Some have said so, but sadly not. Mrs. Gorley does have many obliging servants. A footman found this for me to bring outside when I fled. Only one glass, but I haven't used it yet, if you would care to."

May imagined touching her lips where his might have been and shivered. She suddenly felt so daring, quite unlike herself. "Yes, thank you."

He poured out the golden liquid with one deft twist

of his wrist and handed her the glass. His bare fingers brushed her, warm through the thin kid of her gloves. She took a glorious sip of the bubbling, tart champagne, and then another. It was beyond delightful, not at all like the flat stuff they had at home.

"So, no need for a yacht," she said. She sighed as she examined the far-off vessel, so pale and serene at that distance, so vast and no doubt quick. "She *is* a beauty, though. Two hundred and eighty feet? And no doubt fast as the wind."

"Two hundred and eighty-five." He glanced down at her, and she sensed his surprise. A lady was never meant to surprise. A lady should soothe and cluck and agree with a gentleman as he talked. But right now, in that Italian-novel moment, she scarcely cared what a lady should do. She felt like a different person there with him.

"You're a sailor, then?" he said, and took a swig of champagne straight from the bottle, making her laugh yet again.

"A bit. Not good enough to actually steal that gorgeous lady from her moorings, but I do row a little. I've been coming to Newport since—well, since always. And Mr. Gorley has his yacht, the *American Girl*. He takes me out with him sometimes. It's a lovely vessel, but not like that one."

"You're close to the Gorleys?"

"Mrs. Gorley is my godmother. She and my mother have been friends since they learned to walk. My mother was a Skuytercliff, and so was Mrs. Gorley's grandmother." It sounded horribly snobby to put it like that, and May felt her cheeks turn warm. She took another drink.

He went very still and quiet, and she wanted the teasing back. She didn't want to be a Van Der Berg. She just wanted to be May.

"I wonder what that one is called," she said, gesturing with her shockingly empty glass to the yacht. "I'd say—*Leviathan*. Or *Olympus*."

"She's the *Eos*. Goddess of the dawn."

"You must have sharp eyesight! How can you tell?"

"Because she's mine. I sailed her here tonight for the ball from Manhattan."

"Yours?" May gasped. "My stars. You have lovely taste, sir. Have you taken her far? To Europe, maybe, or even Egypt or India?" She studied his gloriously handsome face in the moonlight, beginning to suspect he could do anything at all.

He laughed. "Who would have the time? Though I admit a look at the pyramids would be grand."

"Everyone I know has nothing *but* time," May said. "And they tend to fill it by changing clothes and paying pointless calls."

"I'm not most people," he said, that accent deepening, becoming almost like a song.

May looked up at him, made bold by the wine and the darkness of the night. She saw his eyes were blue. No, not just *blue*—how dull that word was. They were cerulean. Lapis. So vivid against that dark hair. And she wished, more than she had ever wished for anything, that she could be beautiful to match him. She knew she was hardly hideous. She had the Van Der Berg gray eyes and the Skuytercliff reddish-gold hair from her mother—*We are descended from Tudors, dearest. So scandalous...* She was slim and just the teensiest bit freckled from lawn-tennis afternoons.

But this moment, this man, this Medici, deserved a golden goddess. Someone tall and willowy, with a fashionably grand bosom.

"Indeed," she said. "You are not like anyone else at all."

He smiled at her, a glorious, piratical bright white grin that showed one vaguely crooked tooth. Like the nose, it just made him more perfect. "And you're different from anyone I've ever known. I always thought fine New York ladies would be simpering and shy. But you're smart and funny. I guess it takes an eccentric to know one?"

May was sure she should be insulted, but really she was quite pleased. She *was* different—she had always been all too aware of that in a world that prized only one sort of female. She didn't feel so odd now, though. Didn't feel she was outside something peeking in, always observing, never doing. She was just *there*. Just herself.

She leaned closer and gave him a teasing little smile. "Why, sirrah. Have you perchance been watching me in order to know that?"

"I might have seen you in the ballroom," he said roughly, watching her intently.

She wished again she was beautiful, that she wore some glorious crimson gown, that his glimpse across the ballroom drew him to throw himself at her feet, declaring undying devotion. "You didn't ask me to dance. And then I suppose we both ran away."

A strand of music drifted over the lawn, a Viennese waltz, a bit of sparkling starlight. "We could dance now," he said.

"Dance—here?"

He took her empty glass and set it down on a small wicker table with his bottle. He bowed low, offering his hand. He wore no gloves, and she saw he had long, slim, elegant fingers. Perfect for caressing a lady's bare skin, she was sure. "May I have this dance, my lady?"

"Let me consult my dance card." She held up her wrist and saw she had lost the small engraved card anyway. But she longed to hide her hand, seeing how shabby her glove, a hand-me-down from her mother, had become. She covered it with a curtsy. "Why, yes, sir, I do believe this dance is yours."

He bowed, reached out to take her hand, then wrapped his other around her waist. It was perfectly proper, just like in any well-lit ballroom, but she'd never quite felt a touch like that before. So warm, so insistent. So enticing. They swayed to the distant, imagined sound of a waltz, slowly, learning each other's rhythm and step, then faster, spinning, twirling, until she was giddy with it!

He was not the best dancer she'd ever met, his steps too fast, too broad, but he held her easily, guiding her own steps, and she followed him eagerly. Yes, it was not the "best" dance, but it was certainly the most real she had ever known. The most fun.

Her silk and tulle skirts, the ruffled train, wrapped around them as he swirled them around faster and faster, making her laugh with abandon. The weight of the fabric seemed to be the only thing that held her to the ground. Otherwise she would spin up and up into the starlit sky with him.

Their steps slowed until they stood still, still pressed together. "I've never danced with someone without being introduced before," she said, her voice too ridiculously breathless in her ears. Yet she couldn't help it. Spinning in his arms was the most exhilarating thing she'd ever done.

He gave her that crooked, heart-stopping little smile. "Too bad of me," he said, still holding her close. "I'm Connor O'Neill."

May gaped up at him. Connor O'Neill? So he truly *was* a magician, or so the newspapers said when they covered him making yet another million. *The Railroad Wizard.* She'd read about his companies, railroads, steel mills, stock mergers, things she couldn't really understand yet they seemed to bow to his will. She'd read about the grand house, a palace he was building on Fifth Avenue in the Fifties, shockingly uptown near the Vanderbilts. A whole city block of marble and gilt. She'd marveled at the tales about him but never imagined she might meet him. And here she had danced with him!

His smile turned a bit wry. Cynical. "I daresay introductions go both ways."

"I— Yes. Of course. I'm May Van Der Berg." Was that really her name? She could barely remember when she looked into those ocean-blue eyes.

"Well, Miss Van Der Berg." He took her hand in his and brushed a soft, warm kiss over it. "You know what also goes with moonlight and champagne on the deck of a fine yacht?"

"Seasickness?" she blurted.

He laughed, and that cloud of doubt vanished as his eyes shimmered with humor. "I would say—kisses often go well under such a starlit sky."

May thought again of her books and realized that was exactly the sort of thing the dashing heroes and tragic heroines might do, before they were parted forever. Kiss beside the sea. "I daresay they might, yes."

She knew she shouldn't stay there with him. There was the etiquette of it, of course, but more dangerous, *far* more dangerous, was the way he made her feel. As if her very skin was sizzling with laughter and need. Yet she couldn't give it up, not yet.

She peeked up at him and found that his magical blue eyes glowed in the shadows, so intense as he studied her. Slowly, so slowly she could hardly breathe waiting for it, his lips lowered toward hers.

Her eyes fluttered closed, and she felt the heat of his kiss touch her brow, so light and soft it made her burn even hotter. His lips slid to the pulse that beat at her temple, her cheekbone, making her tingle all the way down to her satin shoes.

She couldn't hold back an instant longer. She stretched up on her tiptoes and drew him even closer, until at last their lips met. A small, questing, almost sweet touch at first, but then something crackled and exploded between them, and so much need and desire poured out. He groaned, and his arms tightened around her as if he would never let her go.

Her lips instinctively parted under his, and he moaned as if in exquisite pain. His tongue lightly touched the tip of hers, as if seeking something, asking. When he found his answer, his kiss turned hungry, frantic, her own rising up to meet it.

A crash exploded over her head, a whistle and crack she was sure was her own heart, leaping away into his hands. But she opened her eyes, tilted back her head and saw they were real, the midnight fireworks at the ball. Red and green and gold, casting light over her dreams.

"I have to go," she gasped, more out of breath than any satin bodice could make her. "My mother will be looking..."

"Let me come with you, then," he said roughly. Was he so affected by their kiss, too? "Some of Mrs. Gorley's lanterns have gone out, and the lawn is dark."

She hesitated. She didn't want to part from him, nor did she want this dream to end in the bright lights and close scrutiny of the ballroom. But he was right, it was darker now on the path back to the house, and she felt distinctly unsteady on her satin shoes. If she was lucky, her mother would be too distracted by the fireworks to remember that May had been gone quite so long.

"Thank you," she said, suddenly so shy. As if she hadn't just kissed him, danced with him, touched him. Found out he was a man much too extraordinary for her. She smoothed her tulle skirt, made sure the wreath of roses still bound her hair. If she was too pink-cheeked now, that couldn't be helped.

He straightened the lapels of his fine jacket, and she noticed that stray wave of hair fell over his brow again. She reached up instinctively to smooth it back, feeling the rough silk of it catch on her glove.

They stepped out of the teahouse, and she realized how late it had really grown. The night breeze was chilly off the sea, the smell of salt and smoke heavy. Side by side, not touching but so close she could feel him there, feel the heat of him and the shift of his graceful movements, they made their way up the lawn toward the veranda.

As they came closer to the house, she felt as if she was dropping back to solid earth from some enchanted star she'd swung on for just a while. She'd been a version of May she wanted to be for just a few moments; now she had to be herself again.

Any vague hopes she'd had of slipping into the house without being noticed faded when she saw her mother and Mrs. Gorley at the edge of the veranda, near the marble steps. Everyone else stared up at the last of the fireworks, wheels of silver and blue, but her mother studied the crowd, twisting the handle of her fan in her gloved hands.

Adeline Van Der Berg, she of the sharpest eyes in Manhattan, saw May at once. She focused her amber-brown eyes on her daughter. "May. There you are at last," she snapped, just as she cracked her painted silk fan open. Even Connor seemed abashed by the straight, piercing focus of her stare.

"I just needed a bit of air, Mama," May said as she slowly climbed the cold stone steps up to where her mother waited like a judging empress. "I was walking in the garden…"

"In the damp grass? And who is this?" Adeline demanded.

"Why, Mr. O'Neill," Mrs. Gorley said sweetly. "Adeline, dear, this is my most prized guest tonight, Mr. Connor O'Neill. Of O'Neill Holdings."

Adeline frowned. "O'Neill? Do we know your people, sir?"

May bit her lip as she realized they were attracting some attention, people at the edge of the crowd trying to stare discreetly to see what would happen when a Van Der Berg met an O'Neill. She wanted to run away into the darkness again, pulling Connor with her.

"Not unless you know the County Wicklow O'Neills, madam," he answered with a hint of laughter in his voice. He bowed, as steady and cool as an ice cellar. He'd certainly recovered his senses from their kiss.

"Mr. O'Neill kindly offered to escort me back to the house, Mama, when I saw him on the path. I hadn't realized it had grown quite so dark," May said.

"So kind of him!" Mrs. Gorley cried. She leaned closer to Adeline and whispered something. Adeline's expression shifted to a small, ever so small smile.

"Indeed. Very kind, Mr. O'Neill," she said. She sounded almost...warm. May was shocked. "We are having a little tea at our house on Saturday afternoon. Nothing grand like my dear Mrs. Gorley's ball, of course—our place is quite tiny. But May and her friends do enjoy a bit of croquet in such fine weather. Do you play the game, Mr. O'Neill?"

It certainly sounded as if she wasn't asking about croquet.

May and Connor exchanged a startled glance. "Very badly, Mrs. Van Der Berg, but I also enjoy a game now and then. As you say, the weather is too fine to stay indoors."

"Then I hope you will join us, so we can thank you for so gallantly coming to our May's assistance this evening."

He bowed again, his expression unreadable. "I should be glad to, Mrs. O'Neill, thank you."

Adeline nodded imperiously and took May's arm. "Until then. We are off Spring Street, the house of Mrs. Skuytercliff. May, dearest, we should be going now. Emily has kindly sent for her carriage for us."

As she was led away, May glanced back at Connor, half-ecstatic she would soon see him again, half-unsure what was happening. Mrs. Gorley held his arm and whispered in his ear, but he watched May, his face awe-strikingly handsome, but his expression blank. Was he happy he would see her again, too? Or angry his little flirtation would not end?

"Mama," May murmured as they took their wraps in the foyer. "That was terribly kind of you. But perhaps Mr. O'Neill…"

"Yes. I have heard of him. Surprising of Emily to invite him, but then again times *are* changing. They say Mrs. Astor will attend Mrs. Vanderbilt's ball this winter season! Shocking, but there it is." She drew her velvet cloak closer and swept out to the pale graveled drive where Mrs. Gorley's grand landau waited. "I do like things that are *new* as much as anyone, May. You needn't look so startled."

Yet she *was* startled. Deeply so. Her mother had never expressed the tiniest bit of interest in anything "new," or indeed anything she hadn't seen and known since earliest childhood. "He was very kind," she ventured. She wouldn't think of that kiss, scared the memory of its heat would show on her face and she would never see Connor again.

"Emily tells me he has some adequate qualities," Adelaide said as she settled back on the fine, soft leather seat, a fur-edged blanket waiting for her lap. She ran her hand gently over the unaccustomed luxury of it. *Adequate* might not seem such a ringing endorsement, but May knew that from her mother it spoke absolute volumes.

Maybe that night didn't have to be a brief fantasy after all. May sighed dreamily and stared out at the suddenly glorious night.

Well. The evening was coming along much better than he could have hoped.

Connor hadn't known what to expect when he received Mrs. Gorley's invitation to her ball. He'd done business with Mr. Gorley and liked the man. He was astute and funny, different from the usual New Yorker of his ilk. No snobbery or stuffiness. He liked Mrs. Gorley, too, the few times he met her; she had a sense of humor, as her husband did, and interesting conversation. And when he mentioned he meant to take the *Eos* on a short cruise, she'd said, ever so casually, "Oh, you must stop at Newport for my little summer soiree! It's all rather silly, I know, but good fun, if I do say so myself. I have it every year. You might enjoy it! And enjoy some of the guests..."

Connor wasn't so sure about that. Work—that was his life. Ever since he was a kid in that dingy room in Hell's Kitchen, working every hour he could running errands for shopkeepers, digging ditches, selling vegetables, begging to learn from everyone he could, he'd thought about little else. Now that his millions were parked safely in banks and ever-growing investments, everyone said he should take time to enjoy the fruits of his labors. Travel! Join clubs! Go to balls! His old friends from his youth had fallen away, distanced by his new life more than the new physical distance of the streets, and he had only his mother and sister. They needed him after the loss of his father, and the more he drove himself the more he felt bound up in gaining more and more. The end of his old social life, his old pals—he missed them, but they hated his new life and were lost to him.

And now he needed to get married. Find a fine lady, a nice girl to keep his houses and give him a family. That suggestion was usually from his mother, gentle but firm and ever more insistent.

He always just smiled at such suggestions, nodded and went on working. The *Eos* had been the only indulgence he made for himself. What else but work

was there for an Irish lad who had clawed his way
up out of the gutter onto Fifth Avenue? What "fine
lady" would have him? The sort of woman he wanted,
kind and graceful and cultured, kept their distance
from him. He'd seen it before. He had money, yes,
but it was brand-new, and he still had a brogue to his
speech. He just had to keep building, keep planning,
keep changing. Keep his family safe.

So he put his mother in charge of his new house,
which she did cheerfully, even though he knew she
hated it—*Such a blessed cold mausoleum, Connor
dearest*, she clucked. And he worked on.

He did take invitations to parties once in a while,
of course. Receptions and small dinners given by
men he'd done business with. But not often with people like the Gorleys. Not that he was invited to such
homes as a general rule. Society hostesses were terrified of Mrs. Astor and her judgments and wouldn't
often step a toe out of line from the accepted invitation lists. He worked with their men, sometimes
sailed with them or went to their clubs, but their
wives were different. Only the most daring wives
had him in their drawing rooms.

Perhaps it was curiosity that brought him to Newport that evening, then. He wondered about such
houses, such women. He wanted to see people's faces
when he strolled into the ballroom. And he wanted

to find a way in for his mother, and especially for his sister. Jane deserved a place in this world, deserved a fine husband and grand home of her own, and he would get it for her if he could.

"You might enjoy it," Mrs. Gorley had said.

He hadn't. The music was glorious, with her three orchestras, and her food sublime and champagne the finest. But the conversation was stilted and dull, the young ladies giggling, the older ladies suspicious. A couple of the more daring debutantes danced with him, though he found *daring* and *debutante* didn't really go together. They were pretty, soft and sweet, but hadn't looked right at him or spoken more than a few words, generally about the weather and the flowers in their silver vases.

And he didn't know what to say to them, either. His own female friends, actresses and demimondes, and the merchants' daughters and tavern girls of his youth, didn't give a man a solid base for conversing with young misses in Newport ballrooms. And their mothers' suspicious little frowns from the edges of the parquet floor didn't help. It made courtship more difficult than closing any business merger at all.

So he'd been a coward. He'd taken a bottle of the Gorleys' excellent champagne and decamped to the gardens. From that fancy little folly looking down to the sea from one window and back to the house from the other, he'd reveled in the quiet. That was one very grand and valuable thing he'd found money could give him. Quiet. His youth had been so full of clamor and noise and violence, his adulthood in the halls of ruthless business not much different, just violence of a different sort. But once a door was closed, whether a large office or a vast house or a fine carriage, there was only silence. A great luxury.

There he could hear faint music, the rush and ebb of the sea, a bird fluttering in the hedges, and he watched the party from that safe distance. He had to admit, ladies like Emily Gorley and her ilk knew how to give a proper party. Three orchestras, servants in powdered wigs and satin knee breeches, heaping baskets of glittering favors—fans, mirrors, cigarette cases. Flowers floating in scented fountains. He had to remember it all to tell his sister, Jane. His mother disliked such folderol, but Janey loved it, devouring the newspapers' society columns every day.

She'd have loved this place, this ball. She'd love to be part of it all. And Connor knew a lot of people expected he could climb his way into it now that his fortune had reached such vast proportions—with the right marriage.

The thought was exhausting. Work, now, that he

could always do. Work all day and night. But court-ing someone like those girls in the ballroom...

Then *she* stumbled in.

He'd glimpsed her in the house. That shining red-gold hair piled high in loops of curls and braids and crowned with flowers, her slim white shoulders ris-ing from a froth of tulle, her uncertain smile as she looked around her. That gleam of something behind her gray eyes, something like watchful intelligence quickly hidden. She was the one he really wanted to dance with, but she'd vanished so quickly. Until she'd appeared again, out of breath, a bit dishev-eled, as if she'd fled from the crowd just as he did. Wide-eyed, smelling of lilac perfume, delicate as a fairy creature.

Yet not so delicate as all that. She'd laughed with him, teased him a bit, drank champagne, danced—and kissed him. Oh, how she'd kissed him!

He hadn't meant to do that. No matter what she dared there alone with him, she *was* a lady. She did share something with those other girls in the ball-room, a softness and wonder that came from never being in danger, never wanting for food or warmth or safety or family. Never even knowing there was such a lack in the world. Her smile was gentle, her touch fleeting and sweet. Her laughter—oh, faith, her laughter. Silvery and rippling, like a song.

Connor had never had time for softness in his life, his work. No time for certainties. Maybe that was why her laughter, her touch, drew him into her moonlight aura so completely. Wrapped around him like a silken blanket and held him fast before he even knew what was happening.

Maybe that was why he'd dared to kiss her. And when he did…

The taste of her, champagne and peppermint and flowers, the way she smelled, the way she felt as her body softened against his and she sighed, enchanted him completely and he was lost. It was gone all too soon, and now he craved more and more of it. More of her.

May. That was her name. It suited her so well. The warmth and tenderness of springtime.

He stared down at the crowded garden now from the veranda, watching her as she vanished with her mother, daring to glance back at him just once.

The mother. That was a funny thing, Connor thought as he tapped his palm impatiently on the cold marble balustrade. He'd expected someone like her to warn him off, as those other sharp-eyed society mamas did, politely shepherding him away from their pale darlings. He didn't expect her to invite him over for tea and croquet. Croquet, of all things!

He'd go, of course. He couldn't stay away from

May, his fairy of the moonbeams and starlight and the sea. Ha! She'd made him poetic now, too. Maybe all those leather-bound, gilt-stamped volumes the decorators had put into his new library were getting to him!

He had to see her again, if only to discover how daylight shattered her magic and he could be himself again, alone. But why was he allowed there at her home? A little old family house in the scrubby fields beyond Spring Street should be even harder for an Irish boyo to obtain than a mere enormous "cottage" by the sea. Yet there it was.

Mrs. Gorley came to his side, all rustling satin and taffeta and triumphant smiles. She tapped his sleeve with her feather fan. "I'm so glad you had a chance to meet May. She is my goddaughter, you know, and a lovelier, sweeter girl you'll never see. I am so fond of her."

"She is indeed very pretty," he agreed, though that word seemed paltry when he said it about her. Goddess-like, stupendous, a distant star.

But Mrs. Gorley, watching him closely, seemed to see all he hadn't said. These ladies were uncanny with their seeming ability to mind-read. Their bluff, shallow husbands had nothing on them.

"But May is special in so many ways, Mr. O'Neill. She speaks three languages, rides beautifully, wins all the lawn tennis and archery prizes every summer, reads constantly! I have often thought the usual life of a young lady in her position, so narrow and dull, could never make her happy."

He thought of her sigh when she spoke of a life spent changing clothes and paying bills. Nothing but time. "Her position?"

Mrs. Gorley glanced over the crowd of her guests. "The Van Der Bergs are a very old family, you know, even older than my dear friend Adelaide's family, the Skuytercliffs. Both of them of Dutch origin, of course. Yet, as I'm sure a man of your astute instincts knows, old names are not always compatible with old—or new—fortunes."

Connor nodded slowly, remembering May's shabby gloves and small pearls. "Are you saying that her family, that her father..."

Mrs. Gorley sighed. "Henry Van Der Berg is an excellent man, quite intellectual and thoughtful, but he does like to read excessively. Spends all his time in his library there in the old Washington Square house, I fear, never noticing if the roof leaks or the walls crumble over his head! They do so count on poor May, so much piled on her shoulders. I would so much like to see her happy. Happy and safe."

Connor nodded again, watching Mrs. Gorley steadily in return so she knew he fully understood what she meant. Safe financially, safe with a firm roof over her head. "She is a lovely young lady indeed."

Mrs. Gorley nodded, and wandered away to chat with more guests, leaving Connor alone on the terrace. He sat down on a cushioned bench near one of the tall open windows and studied the crowd, the gleam of satins and sparkle of diamonds, the smiles and chatter and ease of it all. Yes—his sister would love someplace like that.

And maybe, with such family troubles, May Van Der Berg wasn't so soft and safe as he had imagined. He doubted she knew much about her godmother's, and perhaps her mother's, matchmaking schemes. Other women had sometimes pursued him in the past once he made his money, and they were not subtle about it. Not as unseeing as May seemed. If that was not so, then she was missing her calling as an actress to rival Lillie Langtry. Yet May was still in danger of poverty and want.

Connor felt a flash of something like protectiveness, fierce and primitive. He didn't deserve a lady like her. He'd seen too much, done too much. She was like a warm fire on a cold night, a haven of sweetness. It would be a grave injustice if she lost it in the hardness of the world.

Connor decided. He would go to that croquet game.

The *Eos* wouldn't leave her mooring at Newport anytime soon.

He heard the stiff rustle of silk gowns just beyond the open window, giggles and flutters as two ladies sat down inside, right at his back. He half listened to their gossip in bemusement.

"That gown, Matilda darling, you cannot imagine! Black satin on a young lady in her first season—shocking…"

Was this really the sort of thing ladies talked about when they were alone? He couldn't imagine May being interested in shocking black satin, but then he needed to know her better. To decipher how to win her.

"And poor May Van Der Berg! She is pretty enough, I suppose, but that frock of hers…" one of the gossiping ladies said, all airy sympathy.

"An unfortunate choice. But then Adelaide Van Der Berg must have advised her. An excellent lady indeed, a Skuytercliff, but such taste. My mama always says…"

"At least May is sweet… Everyone likes her." The second lady clucked. "One cannot fault *her* with a thing. Breeding shows in the end."

"Indeed it does. There is no finer lady in New York when it comes to *that*."

"It makes it hard to believe Mrs. Gorley could be

her godmother." Silk rattled as its wearer shuddered. "She can be so vulgar sometimes! Even if her mother was a Peyton."

"That explains it. They say there is madness in the Peytons' blood, but the least said of that the better."

Connor thought that was a bit of too-thick cream, considering these gossipers had just been partaking of Mrs. Gorley's fine champagne and delicious lobster patties. Vulgarity didn't keep them away from her excellent hospitality.

"She even invited that Connor O'Neill!" the first lady hissed. He sat up a bit straighter at the sound of his name. "Shocking indeed. What would Mrs. Astor say of such things? His money still stinks of the printing press it just came off of."

"Well..." the second lady said, a bit hesitant. "They do say things are quite different now. Even Mrs. Astor declares that the Vanderbilts are not so bad as all that."

"Well, who would have thought it of Caroline Astor, of all people! Where shall we be if standards fall like that, my dear? You saw Mr. O'Neill tonight. Quite like a—a pirate."

"Oh. Perhaps. Yes, of course. Yet he was rather—rather..."

"Rather what, Matilda?"

"Handsome. Don't you think?" Matilda whispered.

Connor smiled wryly. He was *handsome*. That was something, aye.

The first lady sniffed. "Handsome is as handsome does, and a fine set of shoulders, no matter how finely tailored the coat they're in, doesn't make up for the lack of family. Who knows where he came from? I mean, can you really see him married to someone like—like May Van Der Berg?"

"Certainly not."

"I'm sure he'd make a good enough husband for the right sort of girl. A shopkeeper's daughter, maybe. Like must marry like, or they will never be able to make a home together. A lady must marry her own sort, or her life would be complete chaos."

The gossips drifted away into the crowd, leaving Connor to his jumble of thoughts. Even he knew that romance and courtship were very different among people like May Van Der Berg. He had much to learn about the ways of this world, *her* world. But he was a patient man.

He rose and made his way down the terrace steps. He was even more determined now, and when Connor was determined, when he really set his mind to something, on a goal, he achieved it. He never rested until it was his. And now he wanted May Van Der Berg.

He was set on winning her, no matter what he had to do. Even if he had to learn how to become a real blasted *gentleman*.

Chapter One

The opera, December

May sat in her parents' box at the Academy of Music as Adelina Patti's voice rose up to the domed ceiling, painted with figures of Poetry, Music, Comedy, Tragedy. They said that the lavish new Metropolitan Opera was set to open on Broadway in a mere few months, underwritten by people like the Vanderbilts when they were denied boxes at the Academy. It was a rather shabby place now, that was true. The red velvet was fading, the gilt dull, yet it was Monday, which meant everyone still flocked there. And May had been coming there for so long, she loved the Academy. She loved the music itself and felt so very comfortable there.

But not tonight. Not tonight in the least.

She twisted her hands in the lap of her pale blue velvet and moiré silk gown, and stared down at the bouquet that rested there. Pink "La France" roses and white lilies, perfectly proper for a young lady. Delivered every morning, a steady delivery from the man who sat beside her. Her fiancé—maybe. Almost. Surely soon. If he asked. If she said yes.

She peeked over at Connor O'Neill. He was perfectly dressed, as always, in stark black and white, another pink rose in his buttonhole. As handsome as ever, with that glossy dark hair, vivid blue eyes, face carved by some master sculptor. Unreadable and remote. As usual.

If he was the man she'd known at Newport last summer, the man who'd kissed her until the sky whirled over her head, until there was nothing at all in the world but him and that touch and that heat...

If it was *that* man proposing to her, she would shout "Yes!" in an instant. She would be ecstatic, jubilant. The luckiest woman in all the world. Nothing else would matter at all.

Nothing should stand in her way. If only—if only Connor was that summertime man once more. She was beginning to be sure she had imagined him.

She glanced over at him again in the amber-pink lights of the theater. He watched the stage with that unreadable expression she had come to hate. His usual inscrutable face. He was certainly just as handsome as he had been the magical night of the Gorley ball. Perhaps even more so—the city gave him more of a chiseled mien, and his eyes glowed a phosphorescent blue. It made that longing so much sharper, more painful. She'd glimpsed something beautiful, enchanted, and dared to reach out for it. Then it just crumbled under her fingertips. What had she done wrong?

She remembered what they'd done together that autumn when Connor wasn't working. He did work so very much... Galleries, teas, carriage drives, all perfectly proper and staid. Talking of the weather and such. Had she said something wrong on one of those outings? She sat up at night trying to remember, to decipher, to see how she could change, but it eluded her.

Oh, she did feel so silly! So young and romantic and silly. No wonder he didn't seem terribly interested, not in *her*. Not in what she thought and felt. And he didn't share his thoughts and feelings with her. She didn't even know how to begin to find out.

As the soprano's voice soared and looped toward the end of the aria, she could feel her mother's piercing stare, her close study, at the back of her neck. May knew, though of course her parents didn't say as much, that they expected Connor to propose quite soon and that she would accept. They gently encouraged his visits, and even more gently *dis*couraged any other possible suitors, even young men of good families they would have liked before. Not that May wanted any of them. No man was at all like Connor... not the Connor she'd first met. Her parents spoke encouragingly of Connor's qualities, his new manners and reserve, his intelligence, his elegant carriage and pair. The grand house he had built. Her father declared he'd heard Connor had a first-class library, the highest compliment Henry Van Der Berg could bestow. Mrs. Gorley said he admired her so very much, could give her so very much.

May thought of her mother's arrangements for New Year's Day, which went on as they did every year. Callers would come by all day, partake of the punch and tea sandwiches and her grandmother's traditional plum cake. Maybe her parents wanted it all settled by then. May knew Connor, as well as his mother and sister, whom she had yet to meet, were invited.

Connor had not yet proposed, and she had no idea if he would. Neither did she know what she would say. He had seemed so open once upon a time; now she was unsure about everything.

She felt she would surely crack and fall to pieces with all that taut uncertainty, like a plaster statuette. Which she might as well really be. It seemed all anyone expected of her.

The aria ended with a great crash, and the red

velvet curtain swept down on the interval. May blinked hard, as if she was suddenly shaken awake, and looked away before Connor caught her staring. She studied the theater around her, the red-and-gold boxes, the glow of gowns and old jewels.

She heard her mother stir, and to her shock Adelaide rose to her feet. When May gaped up at her, she just nodded serenely and gathered her Indian cashmere shawl around her.

"I see Mrs. Fish over there, and I must speak with her most urgently. I shall not be long. Mr. O'Neill, may I count on you to look after May for a moment?"

Connor, who had quickly risen to his own feet, nodded. For an instant, he looked as discomfited as May felt, before he covered it in that inscrutable mask again. "Certainly, Mrs. Van Der Berg."

"Well," May murmured as her mother glided away. "That was odd."

"Odd?" Connor said, sitting back down in the chair beside hers. He did still smell the same as that dream Connor, spicy and clean and delicious. It made her feel sad all over again.

"A lady doesn't leave her box. Callers come to *her*. My mother would never go against that."

He shook his head, confusion drifting and vanishing like a cloud over his eyes. "So many things I do not know."

"Nor should you! I only know them because I've seen them all my life. It's all so silly. I often wish I could stretch my legs during the interval. I also wish our neighbors in the next box, the Sillertons, wouldn't chatter so much during Lucia's mad scene. I can never hear properly!"

He leaned closer, and for an instant she hoped he might sneak a kiss from her. She ached with the desire for him to do just that, to taste him again, feel his heat. Know that her dream Connor was there. But he just murmured, "What other rules are there? Mrs. Gorley did say I could trust you to be my guide in all things of good society."

"Did she?" May said, feeling a touch of disquiet at knowing he had talked about her with her godmother. What else had they said? What did she not know? "I don't know enough of anything at all to teach it to someone else. And I never found a book about opera rules."

"You just know them because they are always there."

That was true, May realized. She did things without knowing why; it was just how they had always been. She wanted to see them now for what they were, to break free sometimes. Do what *she* wanted. But that seemed unlikely to happen now, even as she once dreamed it might with Connor. "Really, almost no one comes here for the music. They come to be seen to appreciate music, and they often rush away before the ending."

"But *you* want to hear the music. It means a great deal to you."

May glanced at him in surprise. He watched her so closely, as if he could read her even as he was a closed book to her. He never really seemed to pay attention to her, yet he saw this one small thing no one else ever had. Her love of music. Her desire to really absorb it.

She remembered Newport again. *Have you been watching me?*

What did he see?

"I do love music, almost more than anything else," she said. "Like novels, it carries you away, out of this world and into something new. Better."

He nodded slowly, his sea-blue gaze never leaving her face. "I understand what you mean."

"You play the piano?"

"Not at all. There was no time for such things when I was a boy."

And no money, either, she was sure. He seldom mentioned his childhood, his past, to her, but she knew enough to guess at how difficult it must have been, and her heart ached for him. Not that he would ever accept her pity; she knew enough to guess that,

as well. "And no time now? You do seem so terribly busy."

"Not too busy to enjoy music, even if I can't play.
Which I do, very much. But I do feel that way, or
something of that way, when I'm working."

"Do you?" May said, curious at this tiny glimpse
into his world. "Business is like music?"

"Yes. It can be tricky to put together, all those
notes like numbers. It can be hard to see the pattern
at first. But when you do, when it clicks together—
it's like magic."

"How fascinating," she said. That word sounded so
fatuous to her, and yet she truly meant it. She found
everything about him, every hidden bit, utterly fascinating. She longed to know so much more. In all their
time together, she knew so little of his inner heart.
His fears and memories. "Is it like an aria? Notes
one upon another, building and building, until even
thoughts and emotions become clear to us."

"Exactly so. Tiny bits of glass working together
making an image."

"Then just as you might like to learn the piano, I
should like to learn more about stocks and shares,"
she said with a laugh. "If I was better with arithme-
tic. I was the despair of my governess when it came
to numbers."

"But numbers are exactly like music, as I said.

Once you see the pattern, the numbers are yours to command. To guide and control. I'm sure trying to be a society hostess would be a hundred times more difficult."

May was entranced by the look on his face as he spoke of numbers and commanding them, the way his eyes shimmered, his lips curved in a smile, and he seemed to forget being distant and silent. It was amazing, exciting.

She suddenly remembered they were not really alone but in a theater with hundreds of people. People who always knew her, and watched her, and whispered and remembered. May leaned back from Connor and looked across at the Fishes' box, where her mother now sat. Adelaide did watch, her fingers twisting on the pearl handle of her lorgnette.

"I know you have sent out the invitations for your Christmas ball," May said. The ball in his new palace on Fifth Avenue, which was all anyone could talk about lately. "Mama wanted to know if you and your family plan to attend our New Year's reception, as well."

"I am sure we will," he said, that mask dropping back over him again. She felt suddenly cold to see it. "It was kind of her to invite us. Does she host such a gathering every year?"

"Oh, yes, it is an old New York tradition. Everyone

calls on each other throughout the afternoon, taking refreshments and such. It's not exciting, but it's what is always done."

A tiny smile quirked at the corner of his lips, crookedly, achingly, but it vanished much too quickly. "More rules?"

"No, not always. Last year, the most shocking thing happened." May longed to giggle at the memory, it had been so strange and wonderful, cracking up the usual dull day.

"A shocking thing in a fine old brownstone? I can hardly credit it."

Was he teasing her? She was sure she caught a glint in his eyes that said he might be. "Not Mama's brownstone, but that of her friend Louise Leydner and her family. Louise's daughter Imogene was being courted by a Mr. Sadler, though I did hear Papa tell Mama that the Leydners should have a care, for Sadler was not a man to be trusted. And we all did know he liked a drink."

"Do your parents trust many men? I should rather doubt it."

"Well—I think they do. Men they know very well. And Mr. Sadler's father was much respected." And Connor. They seemed to trust *him*, even though they hadn't known him long at all. He didn't belong to the Union Club, or the Knickerbocker Club. His great-grandfather did not fight at Yorktown beside some old general or other. Yet they let him sit alone in a box with her.

She shook away her doubts and went on. "It is true, though, that not many care for young Mr. Sadler's close acquaintance, despite respect for his father. He always smells rather strongly of whiskey and is said to lose a great deal on horse races and such things. Imogene seemed to like him, however, and she was sure he would propose to her at her parents' New Year's reception." May longed to hide her face behind her fan as she felt a hot blush creep up her cheeks at the memory of that outrageous, hilarious day.

Connor looked intrigued. A dimple she rarely got to see peeked out low on his chin, and she curled her hands tight around her bouquet to keep from touching it with her fingertip. "And did he? Propose?"

"No, indeed he did not. He arrived rather late, as we were all having the Roman punch, and he—well, he couldn't quite walk in a straight line. Or speak a coherent word. He…" She lowered her voice to a whisper. "He then relieved himself in the fireplace. Mrs. Leydner quite screamed, and Imogene burst into tears. All our mothers ran to hurry us out of the room!" She was still a bit miffed about that, as she had longed to see what happened next.

He laughed, long and loud, that deep, warm, cream-smooth sound she loved so much and heard so rarely. "You mean the drunken boyo pulled it right out of his trousers and..."

Emboldened by that laugh, by that enticing glimpse of her Newport Connor, May nodded in delight. "Let a stream fly right into the fire. Nothing like it has ever been seen in a New York brownstone, you're right! Old Mrs. Sillerton said so, and she's ninety if she's a day and remembers a lot." She sighed to re-member that reception. Every New Year, just like every single day, seemed to pass in exactly the same manner with the same people and same conversation. Such a shocking scene was truly something to savor. Something to remember.

Not like the night she'd met Connor, which was also shocking but delightful and delicious. If only it had not gone wrong so quickly.

"And what happened then?" Connor asked. "Did Miss Leydner marry him after all?"

"Certainly not. She fled the room in buckets of tears, vowing never to love again, and her parents sent her off to visit some aunt in Washington. I think she married some second cousin of hers there."

"And the drunk?"

"Oh, Imogene's brothers tossed him right out onto the snowy street, his attire still in some, er, disarray. No one really saw him again. I think he was packed off to India or something, though I am meant to know nothing about it, to erase it all from my mind. I must shut my maidenly eyes and pretend not a thing happened."

As if she ever could. It was one of the most interesting things that had happened, until she met Connor.

"Not so very many rules, then, eh?" he teased.

"I suppose there must be an art to breaking them, for one does hear such interesting whispers sometimes. Not like Mr. Sadler, of course, but..." May studied the theater. Light caught on a few opera glasses turned in her direction. "Surely some people are able to be themselves and still use the chamber pot as they should."

She covered her lips with her folded fan, startled she'd said such a thing. Her mother would be furious if she heard May say *chamber pot*.

"Don't tell my mother I said that!"

"I wouldn't dare. Your mother is utterly terrifying." Connor leaned on the carved edge of the box, examining the crowd as she had. She wondered what he saw there. "I should like to know all the rules, all the things you could tell me."

"I should hope the proper use of a fireplace would be self-evident."

That half smile, that dimple, touched his face

again. "Indeed. But other things—how to talk to certain people. What to serve at a grand dinner."

"There are books one could buy…"

"Miss Van Der Berg. There is something I should like to tell you. Ask you. Something I've contemplated for some weeks," he said, almost in a rush, as if he had been practicing the words, waiting to say them.

Was he going to say it *now*? Ask her right there? May's stomach clenched with a cold rush of panic. She was not ready; there was still so much confusion. She glanced desperately across at the Fish box and saw her mother had vanished from her seat there. Surely she would return to May in only seconds, and May had never been quite so glad to think of seeing her mother. She knew she had to decide, but not yet.

"Not here," she whispered.

"Rules?"

"Yes. We're at the opera! One must never say anything of importance in a crowd." She clutched at her bouquet. "If it is of import?"

"It is."

The velvet curtain at the back of the box rustled, and May knew her mother had arrived. "The park, then? Wednesday afternoon?"

"Whatever you say. Yes, Wednesday. Beside the Cupid fountain." He straightened in his chair, his shoulders broad and stiff, his stare blank as he looked over the crowd. "You are very right. I must remember to do things properly."

She wondered at those words. He had to remember? Was that what had been happening? He tried to be *proper*? When that was the very last thing she wanted him to be. But there was no time to ask him as her mother sat down in her abandoned seat and snapped open her ivory-handled fan.

"May, darling, it is quite shocking—Mrs. Livingston's new daughter-in-law wore a gown from Worth tonight, and it is utterly and completely *new*. It just arrived last week! She did not let it wait for even a season. We must hold on to *some* standards, I think. Don't you agree, Mr. O'Neill?"

"Oh, indeed, Mrs. Van Der Berg," he answered wryly. "Standards are all we truly have."

Chapter Two

The house was silent when Connor strode inside, as it usually was in the later hours. The few times he was there during the day, it bustled with the impersonal rush of servants, a veritable army of footmen and maids doing... He wasn't really sure what. He spent most of his days at his office, and when at the house in his study, where no one else went.

At night, there was chilliness and silence. He wasn't entirely sure how a house should be, really. "Home" when he was a lad had been two small rooms on Orchard Street, airless and dim, smelling of fried onions and dirty linen, with a privy for a dozen families down the corridor. A mother who cared deeply, but had to work all hours, a little sister who had to be watched. It drove him forward, always forward, determined to give them all a real life, but it was no home.

Later, there was a larger flat, then a town house,

once he'd started earning. He'd built this new place because he saw other men of fortune do so—the several branches of Vanderbilts rivaling each other with châteaus up and down Fifth Avenue, the Astors, the Bradley-Martins. It seemed the thing to try next, the next prize to win. So Stanford White built him a whopper, a city block long at Fifth Avenue in the Fifties, pale Indiana limestone faced with shell-pink marble and slate-gray mansard roof, ornate towers and carved gargoyles and wreaths, stained glass, the sort of place people gawked up at from the sidewalk.

Modeled after the château at Fontainebleau, the eager young architect's assistant had said over the blueprints. *You shall be just like the King of France, Mr. O'Neill!*

The King of France, Connor thought wryly now as he stepped into the echoing cavern of the three-story foyer and unfastened his coat and muffler from the snowy cold. It was surely warmer outside than in there. Not that the King of France would mind such an inconvenience, but a lad from the Lower East Side who could never get warm enough surely did.

He'd told the staid old English butler, Makepeace, not to wait up, much to the man's obvious disappointment. Makepeace's burning desire to run a "proper" household was held at bay by the large amounts in his wage packets, but Connor didn't know how long that would last. So everything was silent as he made his way toward the soaring staircase, with its fruit and vines carvings along the gilt-touched balustrade, its sculptures of goddesses and cupids in niches. His footsteps echoed on the black-and-white-tiled floor until his evening shoes sank into the antique carpet runner on the wide stairs.

On the next floors were everything the architects assured him he would need, the things that Astors and Vanderbilts and Goelets had in their homes. A library with hundreds of leather-bound volumes. A dining room eighty feet long, with two fireplaces big enough to roast a cow and a towering, coffered ceiling. The china room tucked discreetly to one side housed sets of Meissen and Crown Derby and Sèvres behind glass-fronted cabinets. A gallery lined with Gainsboroughs, Bouchers, Meissoniers. A grand drawing room hung with Renaissance tapestries and decorated with chairs, settees, hassocks upholstered in garnet brocade, palms in silver pots. All bought from London, Paris, Rome.

Breakfast rooms, sitting rooms, a billiards room, a dark-paneled office where he was meant to work now. A dainty blue-and-white office with a Marie Antoinette secretaire his mother was meant to use but never did. Dozens of bedrooms, each with a different theme—the Chinese Room, the Lilac Room, the

Queen's Room. And, at the top of the house, a ball-room looking out over the park from floor-to-ceiling windows draped in billowing sea-green taffeta and a gallery for an orchestra. A dripping crystal chandelier hidden in canvas, gilt and satin chairs stacked along the green silk walls. Silent.

It was a palace waiting to wake up, like in the battered old fairy-tale books his sister, Jane, devoured as a child.

A palace that needed a queen to make it a home, to bring life and warmth and music to its endless rooms. For an instant, he imagined May there in the ballroom, smiling, sweeping in a waltz over its inlaid parquet floor, holding out her hand to him. She was the one who would make this place a true home. A true place for the O'Neills to belong.

Connor paused in front of a silver-framed Venetian mirror and tugged the stiff cravat from his starched collar, then rolled his neck to release it and ruffled his hair. He wanted so much to impress May, to see her smile again, her eyes widen in wonder. But now he doubted this house was the way to do that.

The plan he'd conceived in Newport seemed to be working well enough in its goals. Act like the perfect gentleman, prove he was worthy of such a fine lady and win her hand. It had all seemed simple enough. He had always made plans, executed them flawlessly, moving from one business triumph to the next, always a step ahead of his competitors. Finding a wife should be just the same.

And it had been, to an extent. Subtly let the Van Der Bergs, through Mrs. Gorley, know of the scope of his fortune, which he knew they would find of interest, considering the straits he discovered when he'd looked into their situation. Behave in a way that would make them see he could be a worthy son-in-law. Show May he could be correct and polite.

It *did* go well, as far as it could anyway. He was invited to tea with the Van Der Bergs in their faded drawing room. He went with May to galleries and on drives, making polite and careful conversation. Never kissing her deeply, breathlessly, as he longed to do. He was close to his goal now. The palace would have a queen, a fine lady who would know how to bring it to life.

And he would never take a piss in her fireplace. Surely that was one more point in his favor. Yet he had never counted on one thing. That human beings did not always like to follow plans.

Connor reached inside his cream satin waistcoat, the only color a gentleman could wear, and took out a small blue velvet box. He flipped it open with his thumb and studied the large pear-shaped diamond surrounded by sapphires that rested there. The man at Bernhard's had assured him it was the latest fashion, the perfect thing for such a queen.

Now...now he couldn't quite picture it on May's finger. It was true, the one thing he did not consider in his plan was May herself. In the beginning, he saw her delicacy, her fineness, her sweetness, but there was a steel beneath he was beginning to know and admire. A sense of herself she hid from most of the world.

He did think he saw glimpses that she liked him, as far as he could with a lady with her strict upbringing. After all, she had shockingly kissed him at their very first meeting! A wonderful, sweet, transporting kiss he longed for again. She wasn't at all like any other woman he'd ever known. She was quiet, watchful, her lovely face almost always serene. Hard to read. *Crabadan*, but she was so hard to read! He had to act even *more* the gentleman, deny his driving need to hold her, feel her in his arms, to try to win her over.

Yet sometimes he caught a sharper gleam when she studied him across the carriage or the opera box. A searching glance.

Was it time to act? In business, his instincts on when to buy, sell or hold never failed him. Now he had to admit he was baffled. And growing desperate. Every moment with her had become agony, having to look and not touch, the not knowing. The not having. Desperate men did foolish things.

He snapped the box shut.

There was sound along the corridor, a muffled laugh that broke into the glacial silence of the house. Connor turned toward the suite of rooms past the ballroom and pushed the ajar door all the way open.

It was his mother's sitting room, the place where she and his sister usually spent their time, despite all the drawing rooms and morning rooms and libraries arrayed for them. Not that he blamed them. This chamber had all the warmth the rest of the house did not, a blazing fireplace that glowed on the wallpaper of green vines and pale roses, the white-painted furniture, the tables scattered with books and embroidery and china teacups. A little dog asleep on a flowered cushion.

Eileen and Jane O'Neill sat at a large round table by the fire, papers and ribbons and fabric swatches spread before them. He smiled to see them, Jane's dark hair and his mother's silver bent together, their fine silk skirts spread around them, his mother's shimmering gray and Jane's the pink-and-white stripe of a proper young lady. They laughed, the sound welcoming and warm.

"Oh, Connor, darlin'!" Eileen said. "Did you have a fine time at the opera, then?"

"Very nice, yes, Ma," he said as he kissed her cheek.

"Have you asked her yet? What did she say?" Jane asked eagerly. Jane was an avid supporter of his courtship, caught up in what she imagined to be glowing romance.

"Janey," their mother admonished. "You don't ask such things of ladies on nights at the theater."

"Well, you must ask her soon, you silly boyo. We're finishing up the arrangements for the ball." Jane bit her lips as she studied the plans in front of her. "If anyone comes."

"Several families have said they will," Eileen said. "But if your heart is still set on *the* Mrs. Astor darkening our door, Janey…"

"Of course not. Connor's sweetheart would be enough. We are aching to meet her. She is so very pretty."

Connor sat down at the table and pretended to study a sketch of the flower arrangements. He had planned to announce the engagement at the ball, or if that seemed too quick to propose to her there, under the grand frescoed ceiling of his own ballroom. To show her that all of that could be hers if she said yes.

If only he could be sure that was what she wanted. That *he* was what she wanted. She was always too proper, too reserved, as ladies of her sort surely always were taught to be. He wanted to break that down, but the walls were thick and sturdy.

"Show me your plans so far," he said, smiling as his sister eagerly chatted about music and wine and midnight buffets. That was what he truly worked for—his family. He planned to make their way into society for them. To make this place a home for them.

And, he had to admit, for himself, too. Now that he had found May.

"It will be so grand, Connor!" Jane cried. "Dinner before the ball, for a select few. And a midnight supper. Here is the menu. *Filets de boeuf avec pomme surprise. Marrons glacés.* And flowers! Orchid wreaths and roses, palm trees in silver pots. There will be red and gold streamers everywhere, and lace here and here. Oh, let me fetch the other samples. You must tell me if this is the *right* shade of red..." She hurried out of the room, her striped skirts swaying.

Connor examined the menu. He didn't even know what most of those words meant. He wondered if it was what May would choose. Eileen reached out and gently covered his hand with hers. Her fingers were roughened from years of hard work, though bedecked with pearl and ruby rings now.

"My dear boy," she said. "Are you quite sure about all of this?"

"The ball? Of course. You and Janey have done such wonderful things here. It will be splendid."

"We've done our best, with the help of that frighteningly efficient secretary you hired for us. But I was talking about Miss Van Der Berg."

Connor fiddled with a piece of ribbon, not quite able to look at his mother. She always saw right through him. "Do you have any objections to the lady, Ma?"

"Not at all. I've never met her. I've heard she is well-mannered and on many charity committees. And so pretty. Yet is she right for *you*? Would she make you happy?"

Connor had not really considered "happiness." He certainly desired May, he liked talking to her, looking at her, being near her. "She is a Van Der Berg. She would help us in society, make Janey a fine match."

"Surely that is so, yes. And I know Jane would so love to be a part of all that. I want my children to be happy, above all else. Would you be happy in such a marriage?"

Connor studied her carefully. He knew his mother had loved his father very much, had followed him across the sea to New York only to lose him in that accident on the docks. She had always said wistfully she wished he and Janey could feel as she once had. "Ma…"

"I did love your father, though he left us too soon, God rest his fine soul. I see him in you so much. That sense of honor and fierce loyalty. Your hard work. You deserve a wife who will see and value those things, too."

Connor thought of May, of her gentle smiles, her sweetness. What did she value? What did she dream of? "I need her, Ma," he said, shocked at the truth of those words. He had come to need May, to crave her presence. He would do anything to earn one of her smiles.

Eileen sighed and squeezed his hand. "Then I can't wait to meet her. Just be very sure, my dearest, before you give her that ring."

He nodded. He was always sure in business. He knew how to learn what he didn't know, to ponder it—and to move. Surely that would work with marriage, as well. He had to work harder to learn May. "I will, Ma. I promise."

"Now, here is this ribbon," Jane cried, bustling back into the room brandishing silken streamers. "It's crimson, I would say, and this one is more scarlet…"

Chapter Three

May paused on her way home from a charity committee meeting to stand on the frosty walkway and stare up at the O'Neill house. *Connor's* house. She tried to pretend it was an accident she walked that direction, but of course she had gone out of her way quite deliberately.

She wasn't the only one who stopped to gawk at the sight. A couple was beside her, their mouths agape as they took it all in, and children who had been dashing about madly went still in wonder.

It was very different from the old Van Der Berg brownstone, its modest chocolate-covered walls and shallow front steps leading to a black-painted door, lace curtains at the bow window. This was quite indescribable, as enormous as a department store on Ladies' Mile, so covered with towers and pilasters and carvings the eye couldn't stop. And this was where she was meant to live. With him.

Not that she imagined they would often see each other behind such endless walls. It looked like a place where a person could get lost in corridors and chambers and towering ceilings. If only the hallways could be coated in ice, she might skate to find him! May almost laughed at the idea, yet that would truly be her life if she married Connor.

If he ever asked her. The distance between them was one of thoughts and plans as well as hallways. She longed to find a way to leap across that chasm, but nothing in her life had ever shown her how to do such a thing.

She was suddenly jolted from behind and gave a little yelp as she regained her footing on the slippery sidewalk.

"Oh, I'm so awfully sorry! Are you all right?" a lady's high voice, touched with a faint accent, cried, full of remorse and concern.

"Yes, indeed. Entirely well," May answered, brushing at her fur-edged wool skirt. She turned to see a tall, slim lady in fine sables and a small, pink-beribboned bonnet, peering up at her from a kitten-like face with Connor's blue eyes.

May was startled, but covered it with a quick smile.

"I was just in such a frightful hurry, all these packages. And I'm so clumsy at the best of times!" the lady went on, balancing a pile of wrapped parcels in her arms.

May laughed, liking her immediately. But who was she to Connor? For there couldn't be very many people in the world with eyes that shade. "Not at all. I shouldn't have stopped to stare. My mother would be appalled by my manners."

"Oh, *my* mother is always appalled by my manners! She says I gallop about like a runaway colt." She knelt to retrieve a couple of fallen packages.

"Let me help you." May picked up one box, noticing the *B. Altman* stamped there. "They do deliver, you know. No colt service, but…"

The lady stared down at the boxes, wide-eyed. "Do they? Blast it, I should have known that. I am trying to learn all the refinements, you see, but there is just ever so much."

Rules. Rules to know—and to break. "Learn what, then?"

"How to be a true lady. How to pour tea, and dance, and laugh softly, and dress well." She studied May's walking suit and tilted hat. "Like you."

May laughed. "How can you tell I am a 'true lady'?"

"Ah, but you definitely are. I can see in the way you move your hands. What were you staring at?"

"Staring at?"

"You said you stopped to gawk at something."

"That house. There is ever so much to see. The porte cochere, the stained glass. That appalling gargoyle up there!"

"But that's my house!" the lady cried.

"Your house?"

"Well, my brother's, but I live there. I'm Jane O'Neill."

"I'm May Van Der Berg. How do you do?" May said uncertainly. She had wanted to meet Connor's family so much, but now she felt quite unprepared.

Jane's blue eyes widened again, and she grinned. "Miss Van Der Berg? Really? Oh, but you must come in!"

"You know me?" May said, startled.

"Well, not *know*, of course. But my brother has spoken of you."

"Has he?" May said. She felt the tiny flutter of something like hope. Had he said good things? Confided his feelings about her? She wished so much she knew.

"Yes! You're even prettier than your sketch in the papers. Are you coming inside? It's ever so cold out here. My mother is out this morning, but she would be so disappointed if I didn't properly offer you tea."

May glanced again at the forbidding-looking house, feeling quite shy. "I have an engagement soon, I'm afraid, or I would so love to. You must come to tea at my house soon!"

A terrified expression drifted across Jane's pretty face. She couldn't hide her thoughts as her brother did. "At *your* house? At Washington Square? I—I should love that, Miss Van Der Berg, truly. But I wouldn't— That is, we will see you at your New Year's reception, yes? I'm told that it's an old tradition in New York. I can't wait to see it. And you will be at our ball? I've never planned one before—I hope it shall be just right."

"I'm sure it will be lovely. And so grand! How could it help but be so, in such a house? But your brother hasn't— That is…" May broke off, unsure of what she was trying to say.

Jane frowned. "Oh, no. He hasn't boshed things up, has he?"

"Boshed?"

"Done something wrong. He can be such a woodenhead sometimes, it's hard for him to see things beyond his business. You mustn't mind some of his rougher ways. He's really so very sweet, I promise."

Sweet wasn't quite the word May would have used for Connor O'Neill, but Jane looked so earnest and worried. "He is very kind. I'm just not sure what he is thinking about me. No matter what, your ball will be gorgeous."

Jane suddenly reached out a gloved hand, the packages tottering precariously, and touched May's sleeve. "Please, please do come, Miss Van Der Berg. I'm so eager to see you again."

"And I you."

May couldn't help but smile as she took her leave of Jane O'Neill and turned toward home. She did like Connor's sister, her open friendliness, her laugh. Yet Jane's words made her wonder, what had Connor told his family about her? What did they expect from her?

Her mother was right—things had changed in New York since her parents were children. Even since May herself was a child. Stone like chocolate sauce, lace curtains, plain chimneys. New mansions like Connor's sprouted up all the time, pushing out the old brownstones, bringing energy and fun.

But marriage was different. Marriage needed intimacy, warmth, partnership. May only knew one couple who had married across the Knickerbocker-New Money lines, Ruth Livingston and Ogden Mills, and they lived much of the time in California now.

Nothing had mattered at all when May first met Connor. She had loved his laughter, his boldness. The way he kissed her, as if she was the only thing he could see, the only thing he could ever want, just as he had been for her. Now she wasn't so sure. He always seemed so distant, distracted. What did he really want from her?

She had to find out, that was all. She had to talk to him.

Oh, no. She clutched her gloved hands tight in her mink muff. She wasn't sure she could do that. Talking honestly to a man had never been in her lessons, like music and French, and she didn't know how to start. She only knew she had to do it. So much, everything, depended on it.

She took a hansom back to her house, the tall, narrow brownstone she'd lived in all her life, facing the same square she'd seen all her life. It was very different from Connor's palace, she thought as she took in the bow window covered in fine lace, the scrubbed steps, the frosted glass fan over the black door. Could she really decipher how to bridge the gap between them?

She hurried up the steps and through the discreet door into the warmth of the Pompeian-style foyer, the columns painted in muted brick reds and dark greens, the tiled floor that was somewhat chipped now.

Daisy, the ancient maidservant who had also been at the house as long as May could remember and was one of the last staff left, took her wraps and said, "Mr. and Mrs. Van Der Berg are in the morning room, Miss May, taking tea."

"Thank you, Daisy. I shall join them at once," May said, realizing she was quite late. She quickly tidied her hair and hurried through the enfilade of rooms to meet them. They often had tea in the small morning room now, as it was so much easier to heat than the drawing room at the front of the house. Her father was usually in his library, but the tea hour was sacred and he always joined her mother then.

May was so accustomed to her home that she didn't often really notice it. The furnishings and surroundings never really changed, and hadn't since her parents married. Perhaps it was something about the sparkling newness of Connor's grand mansion that made her notice now. The rugs were faded and fraying, the wallpaper long out of style.

She found her parents beside the fire in the morning room, sitting together in silence as her father stared into the flickering flames. Her mother worked on a piece of embroidery, tiny meadow flowers on white canvas, between sips from the Skuytercliff Crown Derby flowered china, while her father read. Just like every afternoon.

"Ah, May, there you are," Adelaide said, pouring another cup of tea. "Did you have a good meeting?"

"Very good, yes." May took her usual seat between her parents and spread out her skirts before taking the tea. She told them more about the meeting, of the

Junior Ladies of the Academy of Music and the benefit concerts they were arranging.

"The dear old Academy," Adelaide sighed. "I fear its days are quite numbered once that grand new place opens on Broadway next year. I hear they have engaged Nilsson to sing the debut. The money those Vanderbilts and Goulds have to just toss about!"

"Sad indeed," May's father said, turning the page of his book with a crackle. "The acoustics at the Academy are superb."

Adelaide frowned at him. "Yet you haven't been there to appreciate them in years, Henry. Mr. O'Neill, luckily, was an attentive escort. I'm sure we will be able to rely on him in the future, once a certain event has occurred." She put a thin slice of bread and butter on a flower-painted plate and passed it to May. "I daresay he might even buy one of the boxes at the new Metropolitan!"

May fidgeted in her sagging chair. "Mama. I am not sure— That is, I think…"

Adelaide turned her frown onto her daughter. "What is it, May?"

"I know you think that Mr. O'Neill is my most promising suitor. But I am not so certain of him."

"What?" Adelaide cried. Her embroidery fell from her hands, her famous composure for once quite ruffled. It startled May. Even her father took off his spectacles and stared at his wife. "Has he expressed doubts? Have you given him reason to back away, then, May?"

"No, Mama! That is, I'm not sure he ever moved forward in order to back away."

"What do you mean? He has been most attentive this autumn."

Attentive, yes, but May feared his attentions had been so very…automatic. So far from what she had dared to hope at first. "I did nothing to make him turn away," she said, though she wondered if that was true. She had little experience of courtship, and none at all of kisses like Connor's at Newport.

"I should hope not," Adelaide said with a sniff, picking up her sewing from the frayed carpet. "We are relying on you, May. On him."

"Relying?" May choked.

"Adelaide…" her father said.

"No, Henry, May is an adult now. You've seen what this house is like, May. The things we have sold, the things we lack. You must know what a good marriage would mean, for all of us. For your future."

"But, Mama, how can I marry him if he doesn't care for me?" May whispered, feeling suddenly so adrift from everything that once seemed so solid.

"Care for you? Of course he does. How could he not? You are pretty, and kind and intelligent. You have the means to help him on his rise in society. And obviously he can take good care *of* you." Adelaide's harsh expression softened as she leaned forward to touch May's hand. "You cannot help your family, your future children, through romance, my dear. Only through marriage can you be safe, as vulgar as it is to say that. Mr. O'Neill is a good man. I can see it. Heaven knows, he is a handsome one. And his money will make you *safe*. Make all of us safe. You can sand down his rough edges. A good wife always advises her husband on how to dress, how to dine, on music and art, correct forms of address..."

But those "rough edges" were exactly what May liked most about Connor. The way he kissed, the way he touched her. She longed for it all so much.

Wednesday. She was meant to see him again on Wednesday. One way or another, she had to find a way to speak to him honestly. To decide what she needed to do. And oh, how she dreaded it.

Chapter Four

Connor studied himself in the tall, gilt-framed French mirror in the foyer, making sure his dark gray frock coat, his black waistcoat, the pink rose in his buttonhole were all correct. He had no idea what would happen today. And he hated that feeling.

In business, of course, the biggest rewards came on the biggest gambles. Connor was good at that, at following his instincts to make the right investment at the right moment, to see what people needed before they did. But with May, he had no instincts at all. He had nothing. He was stumbling blindly, seeking something in the darkness that he craved so very much.

And he did crave May. Too much. He'd held back so long for fear of scaring her, or driving away her family, whose approval he so much needed. What if he showed himself as he was, a bold boyo of the streets, and they tossed him out? Never to see May again. He longed for her beauty, her smiles, her funny conversation. Longed for her to like him. He'd never been a man who needed connection at all, or even thought about such a thing. Now, with May, he longed for it. Longed to know her and have her know him.

With May, with May. It was all he ever thought about now, neglecting even his business offices. He did crave connection with her, to have her see him as he was. And he didn't know how to begin to achieve that. Now, with the most important thing, after a career of almost never putting a foot wrong, he found he had somehow fumbled. Badly.

Perhaps he never deserved that connection at all. He had cut himself off from it.

He heard a soft footstep and glanced in the mirror to see Jane coming up behind him, her pale blue skirts glowing in the shadows.

"Your cravat is all crooked," she said with a tsk, and reached up to fuss with it. "So silly, Connor! This is not at all like you to be so careless with your clothes. Or careless with anything."

He smiled. She was right; he had worked hard to find just the right attire for a gentleman. To impress May and her friends and family with his plan to be the perfect, aloof suitor. His sister bit her lip as she retied the cravat. Dear Jane, with her enthusiastic ways and sunny smiles. He remembered he needed

May Van Der Berg not just for himself, but for Jane and their mother, to give them the life they deserved. Being attached to an old family name would open doors for them that not even his money could unlock, could introduce them to better sorts of people. Give Jane such choices in her husband. He had the coin, but the Van Der Bergs had the patina of respectability that could not be bought.

"I must have been distracted," he said.

She brushed her palms over the velvet lapels of his coat. "Distracted by the lovely Miss Van Der Berg?"

"Certainly not. By the new railroad deal."

"Mmm-hmm." Jane did not seem convinced. "I saw her, you know."

"You saw Miss Van Der Berg?" he asked tightly. "Where? What did she say?"

"Here. Well, not *here*, just outside on the walkway. Looking at the house. I asked her in…"

"What did she say? About the house. Did she seem to like it?" Connor demanded, feeling uncharacteristically anxious. He liked control; if she saw his house without him there, would she view it as she was meant to?

Jane frowned in thought. "I couldn't really tell. She looked…thoughtful. Watchful. Just like you."

"She usually does look thoughtful." And he wished he could read her. Yet she was not a stock report.

"She is ever so pretty, isn't she? And kind. I bumped right into her, I'm afraid, and dropped my parcels, and she just laughed and helped me pick them up. Not like those other Knickerbocker sorts I see on Ladies' Mile." She pretended to stare down her nose, a disapproving dowager. "You should bring her to meet Ma."

"Should I, then?"

"You're going to ask her to marry you, aren't you? I'm quite sure that great, hulking ring isn't meant for Ma or me, and Miss Van Der Berg is the only respectable female I've known you to pay attention to. And she's coming to our ball."

Connor felt wrong-footed all over the place that morning, especially by Jane. She was always galloping about exuberantly. It was easy to forget how observant she was. "Where did you…"

"It was in that parcel from the jeweler you sent with Ma's new pearls. I put it back before she could see it and ask questions."

"Thank you for that, Janey. I don't want to tell her for sure until I'm certain of Miss Van Der Berg."

"Quite right. Ma would be furnishing the nursery at once." Jane picked up his hat and brushed it off before she handed it to him. "She does so much want you to be happy, Connor. We both do. You work so very hard, and you need…"

"I work hard for *us*. Look where we started, and where we are now."

Jane glanced around, as if seeing not the marble and gilt and tapestries, the masses of hothouse roses and the Bouguereau painting, but the peeling wallpaper on damp walls, the dirt and grime and broken window of his childhood home. "I know, and you are a genius at what you do. But that doesn't mean you shouldn't have someone to share it all! A family, a wife…" She broke off, her eyes going wide. "Wait. You said you want to be sure of Miss Van Der Berg? Are you not, then?"

"I am sure of my feelings for her." And he was. He had been sure ever since she'd stumbled into that teahouse, all cream tulle and red-gold hair and laughter.

"But she is not sure?"

"To tell the truth, Janey, I don't know what she thinks. She seems to like me well enough, or at least she goes along when I invite her for a drive or to the opera. She's just so very hard to read. Like one of the Latin tomes that decorator insisted on putting in the library. She'd make a fortune in business—no one would ever know which way she'd go until she crushed them."

Jane looked appalled. "Romance isn't business!"

"Marriage can be, though."

"Connor. If you don't feel *romantic* toward her, you shouldn't be doing this! I only met her that once, but she seemed so kind and lovely. She deserves better than a business deal. *You* deserve better."

Connor kissed her forehead and gave her a little shake. "Janey! I do care about May. Too much, maybe. I admit I am a bit lost with all of this. I want so much to impress her, and I have no idea how."

"How could you help but impress her? You are handsome, and good-hearted, and heaven knows you're rich. Even if you are stubborn as a mule."

"Maybe that's the problem."

"The stubbornness? Yes, I should say so."

"The being rich."

"Being rich is a problem?" Jane gave a little snort, one which surely Mrs. Astor would never approve. "How could that be a problem?"

"I don't know how to court a Van Der Berg properly. I have the sense I'm doing it all wrong."

"What do you do, then?"

"I try to be an upper-class gentleman. A real toff. Quiet and polite. I heard these two fine ladies at the Gorley ball say a lady must marry her own sort, and I knew I had to become her sort."

Jane shook her head, her eyes squeezed shut as if she couldn't bear to look at his stupidity. "Oh, Connor. Connor! You idiot. No woman wants some aloof gentleman to put her on a pedestal. She wants love. To know she is loved!"

"You think I made a mistake?"

"An enormous one! Eejit. No wonder she won't open up to you."

Connor realized she was right. He should have seen it all along. May was different; he knew that. She wouldn't want a cold exchange, money for old name. She wanted to be liked, admired, for herself. Just as he could now see only herself, her smile, her kindness, her shrewd flashes of intelligence. Surely what she wanted, needed, was different, too. He *had* been an eejit. "I must change my strategy."

"Immediately! At once. If you haven't lost her already." Jane sat down hard on a satin chair by the mirror, still shaking her head. "I may only know romance from books, but I am a female, and a woman needs to feel wanted. Adored. Desired for herself alone. You have to convince her she is the only lady for you in the whole world."

He sat down on the bench beside her chair. He felt more uncomfortable that he ever had, knowing he had misjudged something so vital. "What should I do?"

Jane tapped thoughtfully at her chin. "Well, first get some flowers to take with you today. Not fine roses from the florist. Something special. Something like her. Take her someplace fun, show that *you* can be fun as I know you can sometimes. Then I think you should write to that godmother of hers, the one who introduced you, and ask her to help you set up a gorgeous evening..."

May was early to her meeting with Connor, and she was glad of it so she could let the fresh, cold air start to clear her thoughts. She hadn't been able to sleep last night, trying to think of exactly what to say, what to do. It had all eluded her, and she was no more certain now than she had ever been.

She'd always loved that bit of Central Park, with its fountain and rows of benches, children dashing around just beyond the trees. It was hidden there, quiet. The night's snowfall, so new it was still pure creamy-white and sparkling like tiny diamonds in the sunlight, muffled the noisy city beyond and made things strangely calm and peaceful. She still heard the shriek of children sledding nearby, the clatter of hoofs and wheels from the street, but it was all so muffled and distant.

Usually she would feel excitement for the holiday building inside of her now. She'd always loved Christmas, the greenery and piney scent of it all, the ribbons and tinsel and presents, the music and plum puddings. Now, though, she just felt nervous, anxious, so terribly unsure. As if she would leap right out of her skin and fly away.

She paused under a towering, empty-limbed tree and tucked her hands deeper into her mink muff. That was just how she'd felt when Connor kissed her at the ball. Not herself. Soaring free. Surely that man was still in there someplace? That man she could be daring for. She was sure of it. But how could she find him?

She glimpsed him making his way toward her along the frosty pathway, and her heart ached at the sight. He was so beautiful, in his sweeping black coat, his dark hair tousled in the wind. The whole world narrowed to only that one point that was *him*, as if a sunbeam danced over him while everything else was in shadow.

May nearly lost all the courage she had carefully gathered to say what she had to say. She clutched at it tightly, for so very much depended on it.

"Miss Van Der Berg," he said as they met beneath the tree. She did so wish he would call her May once more. He gave her a low bow, looking so serious, and offered her a bouquet. Not the usual La France roses and lilies, but a bunch of holly and ivy tied with a wide red ribbon. The perfect thing for Christmas. "I hope I'm not late. I wanted to get these from the garden."

May slid one hand from her muff to take the greenery. Their fingers brushed, heated and sparking even through their gloves. "Not at all. I was quite early. These are lovely. I do enjoy snow like this, don't you? All new and bright and fresh." And she was babbling. She bit her lip to stop.

He looked about, as if he had never really noticed the snow before. Maybe he hadn't. Maybe he was at work all the time. "You're right. Nature's beauty is always the finest. Shall we walk a bit? Take it in?"

"Of course." They fell into step on the pathway, silent for a moment. Together but too far apart.

"What did you wish to speak to me about, Miss Van Der Berg?"

So this was the moment. May drew in a deep, steadying breath, only to find she didn't know how to begin. "I—I just wanted to say, Mr. O'Neill, I have no wish to make you unhappy. So we can't continue this way, I know."

"This way?" He studied her closely with those summer-blue eyes. So handsome, but so quiet.

"With—with seeing each other, I mean. I don't know, that is…" She broke off, feeling so silly.

He finally did something. He smiled. The wide, white, dimpled smile that made her heart patter frantically, made her lose her breath. "My dear Miss Van Der Berg. May. We're alone here. We're not in a fine drawing room. You can tell me. I want to know what you're thinking. I always want to know."

May was amazed. She'd expected him to nod and walk away. Not say he wanted to know what she thought. "I should have spoken sooner. Have said that maybe we don't suit."

"Why didn't you?"

May clutched at her Christmas bouquet. "I guess I kept thinking about that ball in Newport."

"I think of it, too."

She was amazed all over again. It felt like this conversation was a winding maze, each turn a surprise. "Do you?"

"Yes. It was a gorgeous evening."

"I suppose I kept hoping we could be like that again."

"I'm afraid I behaved that evening in a way that would be ungentlemanly in your world."

"But that was why it was so lovely! I liked it. Liked *you*," she blurted. She shook her head, her thoughts whirling around wildly. "Why would you want to spend time with someone like me?"

He looked stunned. "What man would not? You are— You're very beautiful." His voice was rough, his accent thicker, more musical.

May couldn't help but be flattered, but she also wondered if her face was all he saw. Did he think she was dull-witted? "Many ladies are far more beautiful than I am, for I know myself enough to see I am only passably pretty. They would be eager for your company."

"You underestimate yourself greatly, but I assure you it's not just your stormy eyes and glorious hair. It's your kindness. Your thoughtfulness. The way you see the humor in things."

"Do you truly think that?"

"Of course, and so much more. I think about you all the time. I am many things, Miss Van Der Berg, and admit I can be ruthless in business. But I am always honest."

Yet another thing she admired about him. "As am I."

"Then tell me. Is there someone else, perchance?"

He'd surprised her again. "Not at all."

"Then I hope you can give me another chance to stop being a fool, Miss Van Der Berg. May."

And there it was. The sound of her name in his voice again, like a song on a summer breeze. If he kept saying it, she knew she'd give him anything. "Another chance?"

"To prove to you I can be worthy. To win you."

The bouquet slipped from her suddenly numb hands, and she scooped it up, shaking. "Mr. O'Neill.

Connor. What would you have done if I wasn't a Van Der Berg, but a— Maybe a shopkeeper's daughter?"

He nodded, as if he could see her meaning. "Please, May. Give me this Christmas season to prove to you how different I can be," he said hoarsely. He was still close to her, all warmth and that lovely, spicy, clean scent. All safety and excitement at the same time.

May stared up at him, dazed. Unsure. Ladies in her position never really married for love, but for position and alliances and fortunes. If she was lucky, there could be fondness and respect. May had grown up trying to be resigned to such a thing. Now, looking at Connor in that sparkling winter sun, she dared to hope there really might be more. If she was brave enough to reach for it.

She nodded. "Yes. Christmas."

Chapter Five

The day was cold but crystal clear at the park when May made her way toward the skating pond to meet Connor. She'd no longer been surprised her parents let her meet him; she knew their hopes now. Marriage, and the path to save them. She *was* surprised Connor invited her skating, though. It seemed that he meant to keep his word, a courtship before Christmas.

She paused at the turning of the path to adjust her skates over her shoulder and gaze up into the pale pearl-blue sky. That morning's snowfall had stopped, and the sky shimmered with drifting white clouds. Her breath came in cold puffs, and her boots slid beneath her on the damp puddles of the walkway. Laughter rang out, caught on the wind from the water, and children giggled as they dashed past her, making her amber velvet skirts sway. They were building a snowman nearby, a towering edifice studded with carrots and chunks of coal, and she could smell the baked apples and candied almonds from the food booths ringing the pond.

It didn't look real, not like an ordinary day but something in a postcard. Or a dream. *Her* dream.

Or maybe she was still caught up in the hazy images that kept her up at night. Connor walking her home after they'd agreed to see what happened between them before Christmas. His arm under her hand, the giddy feeling that she was floating on a cloud, the way his eyes glowed like a summer's day as he looked at her, *only* at her, as he never had before. The shining, warm, tiny point of hope she dared let herself feel.

How she longed for him to kiss her again, pour out such a wealth of feelings and passion and emotion as he once had!

A shout from the crowds of children pulled her back down out of the sky, and she blinked to see that she was still in the park, in the snow and cold wind, and not alone with Connor on a bright cloud somewhere.

She studied the scene in front of her, the laughing couples and excited children, the booths with their cider and sweet treats, the band that played marches and waltzes nearby, their red coats a spot of color amid the cream and ivory. She hadn't been to the pond since she was a child, when her nanny would bring her there if she did very well on her lessons. Since then, she had skated on more private ponds, at her parents' friends Long Island country estates, but this was just as she remembered it.

The paths over the icy pond were lined with fir trees in brass pots, decorated with scarlet bows, to show where it was safe to skate. In between drifted couples in velvets and furs, children in sleds, even a dog that slipped and slid merrily as its owner chased and shouted after it. Smoke rose from crackling bonfires nearby, where people could warm their hands, sip hot cider, flirt and smile.

May didn't see Connor yet, and she was glad to have a moment to compose herself. She knew they'd agreed to learn to be more open with each other, but surely that didn't mean he had to see her all flustered and red-cheeked remembering his kisses! She sat down on a bench to strap on her skates.

"May! Hello!" someone called. She glanced up to see Ellen Driver, an old friend she hadn't met with in a while, gliding past in a flurry of lavender velvet skirts trimmed in silver fox fur and fluttering ribbons. "We haven't seen you in an age! Not since that Junior Patriarchs dance. Whatever have you been up to?" She gestured at a group of young people skating nearby, laughing as they traced patterns in the ice. "Come and skate with us!"

May thought of how Ellen, even though she was funny and kind, did like to gossip with the others, to whisper about courtships and romantic scandals. She'd done so often when May's family's fortunes took a downturn. Once she would have been scared they would whisper about *her* and Connor; now she found she didn't care at all. It was time to mend fences. Was that one way he was helping her? Setting her free to consider only what *she* thought?

"Soon, Ellen," she said. "I'm just waiting for someone."

"Ooh. Of course. *Someone*." Ellen giggled, waggled her fingers and glided away to join the others. They glanced at May, their heads bent together. She just waved back.

"Miss Van Der Berg. May."

She glanced back to see Connor coming toward her along the path. His silver skates gleamed where they were slung over his shoulder, his hands in the pockets of his black wool, fur-collared overcoat in a way that seemed positively jaunty for the formal, watchful man she'd come to know lately. He smiled broadly, that delightful dimple flashing. Her fingers fumbled on her laces, knotting them horribly.

"Good morning, Connor." She slid over to make

room for him on the bench so he could tie his skates. He looked so much different from the last time she saw him, so much brighter and—and was he *smiling*? "You look cheerful today."

His grin widened, white and inviting and slightly naughty. Oh, she *was* in trouble. "How could I not be? We're outside on a beautiful day. I've run away from my desk to meet the prettiest girl in the park."

May laughed, delighted at his teasing tone. "Just the park, then?"

"The whole city. The whole state!" He rose to his feet and held out his hand to her. "Come on, let's skate. I'm not sure we'll have such fine weather for it much longer."

"I'm afraid I made a frightful hash of this knot," she said and held out her foot to show him. She felt terribly daring as she flashed a bit of her white-stockinged ankle and drew her skirts up a bit farther when his eyes darkened.

"Well, we can't have that." He took off his gloves as he knelt before her, his head bent over his task. His touch, those deft, quick fingers, was warm through her boot, the scent of that spicy soap and clean linen delicious on the cold breeze as it tickled at her nose. A longing rushed through her to touch the glossy, gleaming tousled waves of his hair, to caress his cheek and see if that hint of shadowed bristle was rough under her palm.

He looked up at her, and his smile darkened as if he could read her thoughts.

He tied off the end of her laces and rose to his feet. To her disappointment, he replaced his glove before he helped her rise, so she couldn't get just that much closer to his bare skin. He seemed a bit distant suddenly, that dreadful perfect gentleman again. She couldn't bear that. She slid her palm slowly over his, and his fingers closed around hers. He raised it to his lips and kissed her wrist, soft and hot and delicate and shiver-making, just above the pearl button of her glove. His gaze never left hers, those blue depths seeming to touch her very soul. To see everything.

Not so distant after all.

She was quite aware of Ellen and the others watching, but she didn't care one jot. She just never wanted Connor to look away.

His arm slid down to loop around her waist, holding her as close as anyone surely dared in public, and she didn't know quite where she ended and he began. They launched together onto the pond, through the fumbling crowds at the edges toward the center of the ice. At first, she kept stumbling, distracted by the hard strength of his arm against her waist, holding her always safe. It was amazing, how he made her feel so discomfited, so flustered, and so safe all at the same time.

"Has it been a while since you went skating, May?" he asked, setting them into a small, slow twirl.

She thought of saying she had never been skating at all so he would have to keep holding her. "A couple of winters, and not here since I was a child. My nanny would bring me once in a while, if I did exceptionally well at my lessons. I always loved it so much! To fly free across the ice. And there was this one time…"

"One time?"

"It's so funny, I haven't thought about it in an age. One time my father brought me here. He was usually, *is* usually, so caught up in his books and studies, he seldom ventured anywhere with me. It was wonderful! He carried me on his shoulders so I could see all the skaters, helped me build a snowman, showed me how to make a figure eight on the ice. I was surprised he was such a good skater."

"It was only that once?"

"Yes. Outdoor games aren't my father's forte. I wonder why he came that day."

"You care about your father."

May blinked in surprise. Of course she cared about her parents; respect for family was vital in her world. Her parents were kind, caring. But it was a distant sort of love, of respect, not the kind where they could run into each other's arms, giggling, cuddling. "Certainly I do. He is a good man. Yet he's always so busy in his library. I seldom saw him when I was a child, but surely that's true of everyone I've always known. I was brought to see him and my mother every day at teatime, and he would sometimes read to me then. My mother I saw more often. I suppose she was unusual that way! We would sometimes go shopping, or driving in the park, or wade in the sea when we were at Newport. And I always had kind nannies and competent governesses, not like some of my friends."

"It doesn't sound like much to build affection on," he said thoughtfully.

"It was the usual thing." May thought about that—the usual thing. The things that her mother, her grandmother, probably her great-grandmother thought and did. What did *she* want now? What sort of mother would she wish to be?

She was startled by a sudden thought. One day Connor would be a father, too. Possibly the father to *her* children. What would he expect? What would he want from his family? Would he hide from the children in his office, a distant, slightly frightening figure of respect?

"I should like to spend much more time with my children, if I had them," she dared to say. To even hint of offspring would be shocking to her mother, but the new May who was peeking out knew that it had to be said. She had to know what her family would be like, one day. She gestured toward a small girl, bundled warmly in white furs, being pushed in a little sled over the ice by her father. She shrieked with laughter, waving her little mittened hands, and made her father laugh, too. The two of them so carefree, so filled with joy at being together.

Connor looked wistful as he watched them, too. "So would I. Surely a family should be something to enjoy, if a person is so lucky?"

So perhaps he would not work all the time, as she was sure he did now. They could learn to see the world with new eyes together. "What about your own father?"

A shutter seemed to fall over his expression, and he glanced away from the father and child. "I barely remember him. He died not long after my sister was born, barely a year after we came to New York. An accident on the docks where he worked. I do remember his laugh, though, so big and booming and full of joy. How he and my mother would hold hands when they walked down the street. That's all, really. Not much to build an image of fatherhood on. I've had to take his place, protect them. They rely on me."

May's heart ached to think of it. "I'm so very sorry."

"Well, I've seen enough of what *not* to do as a father, and that's for certain. Too many men neglect and abuse their children, and I vow never to be like that. My children will always be able to rely on me, confide in me," Connor said tightly. He twirled her in a wide circle, and when she came to face him again, he smiled, his whole mien different. Sadness cast away. "But come, May, this is meant to be a fun day! A proper courtship, remember?"

How could she forget? It was all she wanted.

He spun her in a loop, faster and faster, making her laugh helplessly as the pond blurred around her, the people and trees and diamond-bright ice swirling. She pushed off from him and tried to trace a pattern, as her father had shown her so long ago. Back and forth, turn and turn, like a dance.

"Oh, look at you! And you said you hadn't skated in a long while," Connor called, laughing as he circled her. He surprised her, too, spinning in an elaborate top-like movement, swift and deft.

"And so are you! You must get out from behind your desk sometimes."

"A man needs fresh air once in a while, as my sister is always pestering me."

"May! How beautifully you do that," Ellen called

out suddenly, floating toward them like a lavender-and-silver cloud, her blond curls bouncing. The others followed her, all of them watching May and Connor with wide eyes. "Come and skate with us. Bring your friend, too!" She lowered her voice and whispered, "Annabelle thinks he's ever so handsome..."

Of course Annabelle would, May thought indignantly. Every woman would. But by some miracle, he was there that day with *her.* "Very well!" She grabbed Ellen's hand and they spun out together, giggling like they were children again until May was giddy with the unexpected fun of it. She hadn't realized how much she missed *fun* lately, worrying about her family. Everything in that moment—her friends, the beautiful pale sky, the chilly wind, the rush of the city and especially Connor, watching her with his gorgeous eyes as if all he could see was her, it all seemed perfect. An instant frozen inside a crystal globe, which she could take out and remember when it was gray and gloomy. Others joined her and Ellen in a star on the ice.

On a spin, she glanced back over her shoulder at Connor. To her surprise, he looked a bit... Was it sad? Not hard or angry, or coolly amused at such silly high jinks, just so very wistful. As if fun was foreign to him. She felt a sudden sharp pang for him, and longed to make him laugh again.

"Come, join us!" she called to him and held out her free hand.

"Yes, do join us, Mr. O'Neill!" Ellen added. "We need someone who is strong and brave, not like these chickens here." Her many suitors protested.

Connor smiled, that bright, teasing grin May had come to love so much, wait for so eagerly, and grabbed May's hand. He let her draw him into their merry little circle, and she smiled up at him.

"Everyone hold on to me and make a line," one of Ellen's swains commanded, and they all fell in behind him, a crooked, wobbling sort of line that would never work in Dodsworth's Dancing School.

May felt Connor's hands close tight around her waist from behind her, so close and warm and safe. She heard him laugh near her ear, like the sweetest music, and the glow of it poured over the whole day, making it golden.

They all slid over the ice, lashing around, snapping back together, faster and faster, everything a blur. May laughed more than she had dared in years, laughed until she was hoarse, and she knew she wouldn't want to let "fun" escape her again. Nor would she let it escape Connor. They could make their own rules now.

The band slid from a merry mazurka into a slower,

romantic waltz, much like the one playing on that night in Newport.

"Shall we?" Connor said with a bow, as if they were in a grand ballroom.

May still felt the fizz of that energy inside of her, that exciting toss of exhilaration that being near Connor brought. "Thank you, good sir," she said, and gave a wobbling curtsy, nearly toppling over until he caught her up with a laugh.

His arm came around her back, and the other stretched out to take her hand. He drew her close, so much closer than they would have dared in that ballroom she imagined. Even through the wool and velvet and furs, she was achingly aware of the hard length of his body against hers. So strong and heated, fitting perfectly to her as if they'd always been just like that.

They spun slowly at first, finding their balance together, gentle, lazy, laughing circles that made her feel as if she was floating up and up in his arms, just like their dance at Newport.

He laughed, too, and lifted her into the air, spinning her around and around. The snow drifting from the trees, the pale dazzle of the sunlight, the other skaters—it was all a rainbow wrapping around her. She held on to him tightly, her one still, strong point.

The band's song slowly wound down, and Connor

slid her to her feet along the length of his chest, holding on to her until she was steady on her skates, the pearl-blue sky going still. She clutched him close as she peeked up at his face, shadowed by the brim of hat. He watched her, too, that quiet, steady look that made her sure he must see everything hidden deep in her heart, every secret hope, yet giving none of his own away.

"Have I got a smudge on my face?" she whispered.

"Not at all," he said hoarsely, his intent gaze never wavering from hers. "I was just…that is…you are so beautiful."

May was overwhelmed by the heat and emotion in those few words, the wonder in his eyes. She was sure he would kiss her again. His lips even lowered, just a fraction, toward hers, his breath touching her cheek, and she shivered with the desire of it all.

"You're cold," he said, and to her dismay stepped back, becoming all efficiency again, all mystery.

"No, not at all," she protested, but he had taken her arm and was guiding her back to the edge of the pond. Once the warmth and shelter of his body, the utter distraction of it, was far from her, she did feel the cold. But not just from the wind. From losing that kiss she wanted so very much.

She sat down on the bench and watched as he knelt to unfasten her skates. The day was surely nearly over, and she feared she might cry to watch it drift away into her memory.

"I should escort you home," he said. "I've kept you here too long."

May didn't want to let go of him yet, let go of their time together, to walk alone to her quiet room in the quiet old house and just have her daydreams of him. She knew she would replay every word, every gesture of the day, holding them close.

"Perhaps we could find a tea shop?" she said hopefully. "Someplace close by, where we could have something warm to drink and just…talk?"

There was a glint in his blue eyes as he tilted his head and studied her from under that unruly dark wave of hair. "I think I have an idea."

"Why, it's truly enormous!" May gasped. "Like a palace in a fairy tale."

"I've often thought that myself," Connor said.

She twirled around to take in the foyer of Connor's house, trying not to gawk and gape like a country milkmaid, but she couldn't quite stop herself. It was absolutely awe-inspiring.

She gazed up and up at the domed ceiling three stories above, crowned with elaborate plasterwork fashioned into vines and wreaths and falling blossoms that echoed the carving of the gilt-trimmed staircase that swept gracefully, majestically upward. She thought of the "Pompeian hall" that greeted guests in her parents' brownstone and how it would fit in one corner here.

Her kid boots clicked on the black-and-white tile, so shiny it seemed like ice itself.

"I'm afraid I can't take credit for much of it," he said, sounding almost shy, as if he feared how she would like his house. "An army of architects and decorators are responsible for it. If you don't like anything—if anything shouldn't be to your taste…"

That sounded almost as if he already expected she would stay. That this would be her home. May felt shy herself to think of it. "Perhaps you could show me more."

"Of course."

He led her up that glorious staircase. Like something at Versailles or Schönbrunn, May thought as she ran her palm along the carved banister, watched by the marble eyes of sculptures in their niches. It was as smooth as the finest satin, smelling of lemon polish, almost sparkling under the light from the tall windows. Her feet sank into plush, bright carpet.

They walked through a series of what seemed endless chambers, sitting rooms and drawing rooms, art galleries filled with wonders, a library, a music room. They ended in the largest dining room she'd ever glimpsed, seemingly acres and acres of red brocade and velvet and gold and priceless paintings, with massive carved fireplaces at either end.

It *was* a fairy-tale palace, May realized as she strolled the length of the dining room, taking in the Meissoniers and Fragonards on the wall. And a Rembrandt! A real one! Yet it was all like Sleeping Beauty's castle when they all fell asleep, silent and echoing. It was full of beautiful things, that was true, beauty she could certainly appreciate; it just needed a warm touch to bring it all to life, make it seem like a home. A place for those children to run and shriek.

She hadn't seen a room so far she could imagine truly living in. A place to scatter her books and embroidery about, taking tea with a friend, playing the piano. There was nothing there that spoke of Connor, either.

"It's lovely," she said, feeling him watch her as she examined the red brocade cushions on the chairs. *Lovely* sounded like such an inadequate word for such a heavy load of splendor. Maybe *colossal* or *stupendous*. Just like the house's owner. Connor defied any polite, pale words. "But where is everyone? Surely you have staff. It's all so beautifully kept."

"Oh, yes, myriads of them. A starchy English butler, maids, footmen, cooks. My mother supervises them, though I fear she's rather overwhelmed by it all. Before we moved here, she had only one or two maids in her house, and none at all when I was a child, of course."

May studied the pristine carpet, the sparkle of the picture frames, the perfect state of it all. "She is obviously doing a marvelous job. Look how this wood shines! Not a thread out of place anywhere. My mother was taught from toddlerhood to run a house, but she couldn't maintain anything this grand."

"And you? Have you learned the housekeeping arts from the cradle?" Connor asked, perching on the edge of that glistening, vast table.

May laughed as she studied the carving of one of the two fireplaces. She was sure it had to be an authentic Tudor piece, etched with pomegranates and portcullises. "My mother did try with me, and I'm sure I absorbed something from her lessons. I always would rather read, or run outside to ride or swim, than go over menus and choose upholstery and plan parties."

"Perhaps that's why my mother is always saying I should marry. She'd rather spend her time with her embroidery."

"Does she?" May said, suddenly breathless. She didn't dare look at him. "Want you to marry?"

He shrugged. "Don't all parents? And sisters, when they're my sister. Jane and Ma are very romantic."

She nodded, remembering his exuberant dark-haired sister. "Did they choose these?" She gestured at a series of paintings along one wall, life-size images of knights and ladies in fluttering veils.

"The decorators did. But Jane does seem to like them very much indeed."

May studied them again, and saw they fitted perfectly into the etched plasterwork. "From Duveen Brothers?"

"Yes, how did you know?"

"I recognize the style of their decorations. The best of taste, of course, but…" But no wonder there was no life there, no Connor. It was all someone else's taste.

"What would you do differently?" he asked, swinging one booted foot from his seemingly careless perch on his priceless table.

May examined the room and tapped her finger against her chin as she tried to picture something different. "I would start by installing sliding doors right there, to give this room the right proportions for a smaller dinner party. It's large enough to entertain royalty, which I'm sure isn't always what you want!" She carefully examined. "I would keep those knights, though. And add flowers! And palms in silver pots. More color. Oh, I could have so many ideas!" A sudden crashing noise interrupted her ideas.

Connor closed his eyes and shook his head, as if

with an old exasperation. "I'm sorry. Just when I thought I had impressed you with how orderly and well-run everything is."

May laughed. "Oh, so you were hiding everyone from me?" She dashed out of the dining room, through a pantry where Meissen and Crown Derby china, rimmed with painted roses and gilt, along with cut crystal and silver vases, gleamed behind glass-fronted cabinets, and found that the sound came from a ballroom, reached by a flight of carpeted steps.

"Of course there is a ballroom here," she said, one of only a handful in the whole city.

Connor's space was very different from Caroline Astor's "room for only four hundred" ballroom, just as his foyer was a world away from her parents' hall. It was all white and gold, mirrors on one side and tall windows draped in palest blue velvet on the other, covered chandeliers high overhead in the coffered and painted ceiling.

And all of Sleeping Beauty's servants seemed to have woken up and gone there. They all hurried back and forth, footmen in black coats and maids in crisp white aprons, carrying wreaths and streamers and dusters.

The crash had come from a towering Christmas tree at the far end of the ballroom. It was listing in its large silver pot, and footmen strained to right it.

"Oh, this can't be!" Jane O'Neill cried. She stamped her foot as she watched the near-disaster, and the scowling expression on her elfin face made her look just like her brother. It made May long to laugh. "It must be absolutely perfect for the ball."

"Janey," Connor called, and she spun around in a flurry of blue silk and lace skirts.

"There you are at last, Connor!" she cried in obvious frustration. "This ball was *your* idea. And you just go waltzing off and leave me to make sure all of the…" She glimpsed May standing there, and her mouth fell open. "Miss Van Der Berg! I didn't see you there. I wasn't expecting— That is, I shouldn't…"

"No matter at all," May said soothingly. She'd been taught all her life to make sure people were at their ease, and she could see that would come in handy in the home of the temperamental O'Neills. "I was just skating in the park with your brother, and he suggested we call in here to get warm again. I'm terribly sorry to intrude when you're so busy with arrangements." She glanced around at the chaos. "It all looks so wonderfully festive!"

Jane smoothed her tousled dark curls. "I do hope so. If this tree doesn't topple over and destroy everything! It's meant to look like the Queen's at Windsor Castle."

May handed Connor her gloves and hat, and hurried over to take the lists Jane clutched in her hand. "Hmm, let's see. If we just move this here, and put this there, it should open this space a bit more..."

Connor stared down at Fifth Avenue from the windows of his ballroom, the glass unshuttered for the first time ever to let the moonlight stream in. Far below, the lights of the carriages passing by flickered on and off, pedestrians hurrying past on the walkway, snowflakes glittering as they drifted down.

Yet he didn't see any of it, not the lights or the snow or the crowds. He could only see *her*. May. She was well-named—even on a snowy, icy-cold day, she was springtime itself. Warm and soft and sparkling as sunshine.

He turned and studied the dim ballroom, leaning back on the carved ledge and crossing his arms over his chest. He was in his shirtsleeves, his waistcoat open and cravat discarded, coat flung off, like the laborer he once was, long ago. The masquerade as a gentleman tossed aside. But his home, at least, was that of a gentleman at last, thanks to May.

More than that, it began to feel like a *home*, because of her. Because of the life she brought with her just by walking across the carpets and the marble floors.

The Christmas tree, that absurdly enormous thing

Jane had insisted on, finally stood straight in its etched silver pot, red bows and gold and silver baubles shimmering, ready to be lit up for the party. He imagined it all, music from the gallery, dancers spinning over the inlaid parquet floor, champagne flowing into crystal goblets. Warmth and sound and life in the vast corridors. May watching over it all, smiling, taking it all in. Taking in what he could give her. The house, the music, the champagne—and most frighteningly, most importantly, his heart.

He had until that Christmas ball to make the house into her true home. To make her stay with him, make his life full of that springtime. And he found he longed for that, longed for *her*, more than he ever had anything in his life. What Connor set his mind to, he always achieved. Businesses, money, houses. He seldom doubted himself, seldom doubted his brains and tenacity. They were all he'd been able to really count on, except for the love of his mother and Jane, and they never failed him.

It was all so different since May came into his world. He wasn't sure of anything, not now, when it was so very, very important.

He stalked around the ballroom, stopping at a marble sculpture here, a gilt-and-white-satin settee there, straightening a painting on the wall. Everywhere, already, was May's touch. Her smile, her gray eyes, the

Titian gleam of her hair. He'd been besotted since that night in Newport, he'd always realized that. He'd seen that rare, delicate beauty, the wry humor that lurked under her perfect manners. What he hadn't seen until now, when she so deftly took charge of the haphazard party arrangements right here in his ballroom, was her calm intelligence. Her way of getting things done with just a smile and nod. She underestimated herself enormously.

She would be formidable in a boardroom—he could see that. Polite but firm, charming, decisive. A Major General of navigating polite society.

He saw what a team they could be. Between them, they could conquer anything. All that, and her warm softness he craved so much. She was everything he had never had, and he needed her.

To be sure, he'd been infatuated a time or two in the past. Now he was in love. And his life depended on winning her. Not just her hand, certainly not just her name and connections and breeding, but her heart.

Connor ran his hands through his hair, trying not to tear at it as he faced the magnitude of his task. It was greater than any business takeover. It was absolutely everything. And Jane was right, he'd been a fool to think some facade of aloof gentlemanliness, a cool distance, would win her. He wanted her heart, yes, but all of her, her true self. And he wanted her to want his true self in return.

He closed his eyes, and for an instant he heard his dreams fill the silence of that enormous house. He heard a piano from the music room, heard May's laughter blend with his mother's and his sister's in the sitting room, the patter of tiny children's feet on the marble floors, party chatter in the dining room. May's sighs and cries behind their bedroom door.

Oh, yes. Especially that.

It was all the happiness of his life bound up in the few days until the Christmas ball. He had torn up the gentleman idea. He needed a new plan. A plan to show her his real, raw, desperate feelings for her alone.

Chapter Six

May stared into the mirror of her dressing table as Rose, the young kitchen maid recently recruited as a ladies' maid to help her, dressed her hair, but she didn't really see herself. She didn't see the familiar chamber around her, the yellow-striped wallpaper and narrow yellow-and-white-striped bed, the floral watercolors on the walls she'd had since a child, or the curls and plaits Rose was trying to pin up.

She plucked a flower from the bouquet that was just delivered, white rosebuds, and raised it to inhale the sweet, summery perfume. *Connor.* That was all the card said, a bold, black slash on the fine cream vellum, but it was enough. Enough to know he was thinking about her, to know he had kissed her, held her close. Was waiting for her.

Waiting for her at Delmonico's! May laughed as she trailed the velvety petals over her cheek. She'd always wondered so much what was inside that magical-seeming place, whenever she walked or drove past the glass doors.

She'd heard such tales, of its grandeur and delicious food. But her parents didn't approve of dining in public. Some of her friends had been to the Junior Patriarchs' balls in the private ballroom, whispering of its lavishness. But she'd never dared to think she would dine there herself, not until she was old and gray. Now she would be there—with Connor.

She closed her eyes and imagined him there, how it would be. He always held everyone's attention wherever he went, simply by being *him*, confident, carelessly assured, always at ease. Always making her feel at ease, too. How many adventures they would have together! She dared not even hope for it all, so different from her quiet, circumscribed life until then.

"What do you think, Miss May?" Rose asked shyly, straightening a pin. "I found the style in one of the fashion papers when I said I should help you. Is it quite right, then?"

May blinked and forced herself out of her daydreams to study herself in the mirror. She'd wished she could be a true beauty, as a man as gorgeous as Connor deserved, as his fine house needed. Instead, she was just thin, small, gray-eyed May. She was startled by the sight that greeted her, her hair piled high, her eyes shining and cheeks glowing pink.

"Why, Rose, you are a genius! Quite wasted in the kitchen," she cried, gently touching one soft, perfect ringlet that fell to her shoulder. "How did you learn such a thing?"

Rose blushed beneath her white mobcap. "Oh, Miss May, do you really like it? I've been studying ever so hard. I've always wanted to be a ladies' maid. I have ever so many ideas. This style is called the 'Persephone knot.' I read it's proper for a dinner party. I was thinking of the 'Fascination' for the Christmas ball."

"It sounds wonderful." May carefully tucked the white rose into one of the plaits.

"When you're married, Miss May, and go out places like this every day, can I— That is, can I work for you all the time? My ma would be ever so proud."

May blinked. She'd never entirely considered what it really mean to be "Mrs. O'Neill" of Fifth Avenue, to engage her own staff and organize the house as she liked. Do as she really wanted in life, as she was sure Connor would urge her on. He wasn't like most men; he wanted her to be herself. Fly free, as no else had ever believed she could.

There would be places like Delmonico's every day. Tea at Palm Courts, shopping, cafés, theaters. A golden box at the new opera house! Yachts. Charity committees, whatever she wanted to support. Houses, armies of maids she chose herself. Boxes of clothes from Worth she could wear immediately.

It made her feel quite overwhelmed, nervous. It would all be so very different. What if she ruined it all, ruined it for Connor?

And best of all, there could be Connor himself. Connor always near her, her partner as she could be his, if she knew how.

Yes, she thought with a surge of new confidence. If he was with her, she could do nothing wrong.

The little porcelain French clock on the dressing table chimed, and May was startled time had passed so quickly. The Gorleys' carriage would arrive soon.

"We should hurry, Rose" was all she could say. She jumped up from the tapestry-padded bench and tossed off her dressing gown to reveal the lawn chemise she already wore. Rose laced her into her stays and fastened the small bustle before she opened the precious new cardboard box stamped *Callot Soeurs*.

Both of them gasped at what emerged from the layers of tissue. When Mrs. Gorley first offered the gown, Adelaide protested. Madame Osborne was quite well for them. But Mrs. Gorley had insisted. Who knew what sort of life "dear May" must soon accustom herself to living? And here it was.

Rose held up the skirt. Layers of silk and gossamer, as pale blue as the clouds above the icy pond in the park, caught up with bunches of velvet camellias and bows, slightly darker blue. It was light as air as it floated down to settle around her waist, fitting perfectly. Rose fastened and pinned it in place before taking up the artwork that was the bodice.

May could barely breathe as she slipped her arms through the cap sleeves, and Rose tightened it to hook the tiny pearl buttons at the back. Snow-white lace fluttered, dotted with more velvet flowers, and barely covered the décolleté that was lower than Rose had ever had before. It wasn't like anything she had ever owned. Appropriate for her age and rank, but in the first stair of fashion. The fabric and trim of the finest quality, perfect color and fit. It was exactly what she herself would have chosen.

Which made her wonder. Was it Mrs. Gorley who'd ordered it, or maybe Connor himself?

She had no time to ponder it now, for the clock chimed again. Rose helped her into the matching blue satin slippers and fastened on her pearl necklace, handing her the kid gloves and a lacy shawl and pale blue silk fan. May scarcely recognized herself as she twirled before the mirror, wondering how Connor would see her, what he would think.

Her mother rapped at the door. "May! The carriage is here. You mustn't keep them waiting.

"Of course, Mama." She hurried down the stairs and found her father himself waited in the hall, her fur-lined cloak over his arm. "You look beautiful, my Mayflower," he said, and kissed her cheek. From him, it was the ultimate declaration of fatherly devotion.

"Thank you, Papa," she said, trying not to cry. Rose fastened her cloak, and May rushed down the swept steps past hillocks of snow to let the Gorleys' footmen help her into the carriage. She settled against the velvet cushions and sighed.

Emily Gorley laughed and patted her hand as if she sensed May's nerves. "How very pretty you look, my dear! What a grand time we shall have tonight. We shall have to try the Baked Alaska. It is all the rage. Everything is all coming together so nicely…"

Despite her godmother's assurances, May trembled as she stood on the threshold of Delmonico's. The threshold of a possible new life.

It was just as grand as she'd imagined, all red and gold with silver chandeliers overhead, reflected in endless mirrors that showed the round tables draped in white damask, a central fountain surrounded by banks of flowers, red brocade banquettes, red-veined marble pillars.

"Ah, Monsieur and Madame Gorley! How *magnifique* to see you again," said a maître d' in impeccable black and white, his dark hair and mustache brilliantined to a glossy shine. "Your usual table, *oui*?"

"We are four tonight, Charles," Mr. Gorley said.

"This is my goddaughter, Miss Van Der Berg," Mrs. Gorley said, nudging May forward. "Her very first time here at Delmonico's!"

Charles gave a low bow. "*Enchantée*, mademoiselle. We shall have to make it an extra-special visit indeed. Your party awaits you, I do believe." He gave a secret little smile and tapped his cheek. "I do see now why he was so anxious on his arrival."

A waiter stepped forward to take their wraps, revealing Mrs. Gorley's new violet-purple Worth gown, and Charles led them across the dining room. May held on to her godmother's arm so she wouldn't be tempted to duck her head and flee. It took all her lifelong lessons to keep moving forward, past famous figures, mayors and senators and dowagers in brilliant jewels, to nod and smile.

But she didn't care a jot for any of that when she saw Connor. They had been given one of the discreet red-curtained alcoves tucked along the silk walls, where no one could stare or speculate. She could just be with him.

"You look like an angel," he whispered roughly as

he bowed over her hand, his eyes glowing blue in the pale pink light of the lamp on the table.

"And you look like the wicked devil who is about to drag me down," she said with a laugh.

"If only I could!" he growled as he kissed her wrist, the tip of his tongue just touching her skin in the space between her tiny pearl glove button. She stared at him, wishing desperately he would kiss her lips, too.

"Um-hm," Mrs. Gorley coughed delicately. "Such adorable little lovebirds! Did I not say it would work out well when I saw them together last summer? And I was quite right."

"Now, my dear, don't get ahead of yourself," her husband said fondly. "Remember what happened last time you tried a spot of matchmaking."

May felt her cheeks turn warm. She'd quite forgotten it was Mrs. Gorley who'd encouraged Imogene and her fireplace-abusing beau once upon a time.

Mrs. Gorley let out a huff and waved her feather fan as if that was of no matter. "Mr. O'Neill would never do such a thing, I am very sure. Now, would someone pour us some of that delightful champagne? I am quite parched."

Waiters leaped forward to hold out the gold-cushioned chairs and pour the wine, before Mr. Gorley proposed a toast to "finer matchmaking instincts."

May touched her glass to Connor's and took a sip, laughing as the bubbles danced over her tongue. It seemed as if nothing could go wrong ever again. She always did feel so absolutely daring with Connor, so completely, finally herself. "I don't think I've ever had excellent champagne before dinner."

"Breaking another rule?" he whispered.

"Probably. But I find I no longer care."

He laughed, and made her laugh, too, completely delighted. "Then I do hope we shall break many rules together."

"I daresay we shall."

The first course, a consommé julienne, was brought, and May found Connor's hands seeking hers under the cloth to squeeze her fingers. Oh, yes— this dinner would be different from any she had ever known. Not just the wonderful food—the famous Delmonico's potatoes, artichokes à la Barigoule, canvasback ducks, and lobster Newburg—but Connor beside her, whispering jokes in her ear, conversing easily with the Gorleys about their fellow diners, yachting, music. Delmonico's was certainly crowded, filled with tables of the richest and most famous showing off their gowns and jewels, smooth-gliding waiters moving among them bearing those famous Baked Alaskas. It was better than any opera, but May was aware only of Connor so close to her.

Another course arrived, and Mrs. Gorley sighed, "Ah, my favorite!"

"It is all your favorite here, my dear," her husband said.

"How could it be otherwise! You two should consider having your wedding breakfast here!" Emily declared. May didn't dare look at Connor, staring hard at her silver-etched fork. "It's very respectable now. They have all those private ballrooms, and of course the food is utterly superb. Or is your mother set on having it at your house, May?"

"I—I really don't know," May stammered. She tried to imagine a grand wedding in her parents' small drawing room with a Roman punch and fruitcake. She didn't know if Connor wanted a stylish wedding, with satin and garlands. Or a wedding at all. He'd said he wanted to court her properly, but maybe he had changed his mind now?

She peeked over at him, and to her dismay that old, unreadable Connor was back. That mask dropped over his face.

He couldn't say anything as their dessert arrived at the table just then, brought by Charles himself, who ceremoniously set it alight.

After that grand finale, the orchestra's volume increased from its soft, dinner chamber pieces to the most popular waltz of the day. Through the edge of the alcove's curtain, May saw dancers circling the floor, their trains sweeping.

"Would you do me the honor of a waltz?" Connor said quietly.

May could only nod, not trusting her voice to work quite properly. She took his hand and let him lead her to the floor, making herself keep smiling and smiling despite the stares she felt following them, the whispers.

She swept into the circle of his arms, feeling as if she moved into a safe harbor at last—but the harbor of a most exciting town indeed. She shivered at the feel of his touch through her gown, the heat of it. She took a deep breath of his wonderful, clean linen scent and closed her eyes as they turned and swayed and spun. She forgot everything else but him. The music ended much, much too soon.

"May," he said hoarsely. He didn't let go of her hand, but held it even tighter. "Let me walk you home? Or at least walk for a little time?"

Oh, how she longed to, longed to be alone with him, to try and peek through that mask again. "I should love to. But..." She glanced at the Gorleys, who were dancing now, laughing together.

"I don't think they would mind at all. Shall we break a rule?"

That made May laugh. She did like this new, bold,

laughing Connor. Moments later, giggling and clinging together like truant children, they slipped out into the night. It was all white on black, lacy snowflakes pale as they tumbled down from the night sky past the gaslights. It made the familiar buildings look magical, strange.

Connor suddenly caught her up in his arms, making her laugh all over again, and he carried her across the street to the edge of the park. "We can't ruin those fine shoes, can we?" he said.

"No, indeed. You had better carry me a very long way indeed."

The park was still crowded even at that hour, with people sledding down hills, shrieking with laughter, couples whispering beneath sheltering trees, nursemaids trying to hurry along their dawdling charges to bed.

They came to the pond where they had skated, and Connor took off his overcoat for her to sit down on their bench. The skaters were long gone, the booths shuttered, and they were in their own world, alone.

"Thank you for taking me to Delmonico's," she said. "It was all as I had imagined."

"Did you truly like it?"

"I loved it! The music and food. So lovely. But I imagine you do such things all the time."

"But never as I have with you. Everything is entirely new since I met you, May."

"My life is definitely new with you, Connor! But how can anything be different for you with me?"

"Because you are the most extraordinary woman I ever met," he said quietly.

May's heart pounded. "Am I?"

"I always get what I want, May. I'm not bragging. It is just so. Business, houses, whatever. But now, when it is so very vital, I have so many doubts. I was infatuated with you from the first night, and I haven't stopped thinking of you since. It's so much more now. My feelings for you defy any logic at all. Any of my plans. I am such a ridiculous fool over you!"

May couldn't speak, didn't dare breathe as she stared at him in the snow-lit darkness. His intent, brilliant blue stare never left her, and from the way he watched her, from the rough desperation of his deep accent, she knew he meant every word. This was no game. He wanted her, just as she wanted him.

What would happen next?

"Connor, I…" she began, and shook her head, trembling with hope. Such sizzling hope.

"May. You've made me see the world, not just stocks and ledger sheets, but art and music and the sky. You make my blood burn, and I need *you*. I want to see the whole world with you, give you that world.

Everything is new now, everything to play for because of you."

May laughed and cried all at once, so afraid this was a dream she would wake from. "Oh, Connor," she gasped. "Do be quiet and kiss me now."

It was only an instant, yet to her it felt like a year of longing, when he closed the small distance between them and touched her lips with his. The merest brush, but she felt so intensely the heat of their breath meeting and mingling, bidding them close.

He groaned and deepened their kiss, giving her what she craved so very much. His tongue touched the curve of her lower lip, and the caress tumbled over into a frantic, heated precipice of sheer need. Something hidden deep inside of her for so very long burst free and spiraled up and up into the night sky until she couldn't breathe with it

"Isn't your house nearby?" she whispered.

For once, he looked shocked by *her.* "May. Are you saying…"

"I'm saying, this whole new world is ours, just as you want. Let's seize it."

Chapter Seven

The house was silent when they tiptoed inside, the foyer lit only with a lamp left on the malachite-topped table, shadows thick on the staircase.

Holding hands, they crept up the stairs, laughing together as if they snuck inside a house that didn't indeed belong to Connor. Past empty enfilades of rooms, so different when May saw them filled with servants. At last they came to a chamber she hadn't been in before, a white-and-gold music room.

"Beautiful," she sighed as she ran her fingers lightly over the keys of a grand piano, so much finer than the old upright at her home, and along the strings of a gilt-and-rose-painted harp. She couldn't resist. She sat down on the cushioned bench and launched into her favorite Chopin nocturne. The longing of the music wound its way inside of her, as it always did, and she became one with it and the night that

wrapped around them, made them the only two people in the whole world.

Connor sat down beside her, his scent and heat en-
veloping her. "Exquisite," he said hoarsely.

Overcome with the emotion, the yearning, May
leaned over and kissed him. She kissed with all of her
heart, her soul, and so did he. She could feel it in the
hunger of his touch as he drew her so close there was
nothing between them to hold them back. No past or
future, no society—just their kiss. It sent them tumbling down to the soft carpet, still wrapped in each
other's arms, a tangle of limbs and fabric, laughing
with the delight of it all.

He rolled her beneath him, his lips trailing from
hers to kiss her jaw, her cheek. Every nerve seemed
alive with sensation, with sizzling awareness. She'd
never felt so glorious, so vibrant and alive! So perfectly where she should be. How could she have
doubted him?

His kiss slid down the arch of her neck as she threw
her head back. He traced the tip of his tongue along
her shoulder above the frill of her gown, easing the
edge of the silk lower and lower. May was seized with
impatience, with the need to feel more of him, to see
him, to know he was real and warm and with her. She
shoved his coat away, tangled the tie in her fingers
before she could unbutton his waistcoat and push his

fine linen shirt out of her way. Her fingertips swept over his naked skin, the lean muscles gilded with a slightly bronzed, satiny skin, hot to her caress. She'd never felt so marvelously bold and free!

Connor groaned, rearing up above her to study her carefully, his sky-blue eyes unfocused with desire. Desire—and a glimmer of doubt she longed to push away. Of gentlemanly hesitation. "May," he whispered roughly. "We shouldn't go on. I need you so much—I can't hold back much longer, and the first time you…"

"I know," she whispered in return, desperately. "Please, please, just kiss me again."

And so he kissed her again. There was no art to that kiss, no careful technique or holding back. Just need.

She edged up against a chair so he could unfasten the top few pearl buttons of her gown, ease her skirts up until they fell back to the floor amid more kisses, more touches filled with need. At last, at last, she felt the pressure of him against her, easing inside of her as the books had described. Only nothing could really describe this moment; nothing could have shown her the joy and fear and hope that flooded her through that kiss, deeper, darker, more fiery than she could ever have imagined.

Their kisses, caresses, seemed to go on and on,

perfect, a moment out of all time when they were just together, the only people in the world. Yet there was also a sheer sense of exhilaration to it all she'd just felt with Connor. All they had done. She closed her eyes and smiled serenely, as she turned her head and kissed his damp brow. She longed to say something, anything, tell him all she was feeling. But words wouldn't stay in her mind; they scattered, half-formed, until she could only murmur, "Thank you."

As she drifted away on a cloud of sleep, she felt him draw her near, wrapped tight in his arms, and she snuggled closer to tumble down into a wonderful, dreamless sleep.

Connor slowly, slowly swam to consciousness, through layers of silvery light that seemed to softly drag him up and up through warm, cottony clouds from the depths of sleep. Not at all like his usual great leap upward, eager to get to his desk as quickly as possible. And where was he, anyway? Not his dark green chamber with its narrow bed and bare walls. It was much too soft, much too— And did it smell like *lilacs*?

He blinked his eyes open to find himself staring up at the ceiling of his music room, painted with scenes of the Muses gazing down at him. And he knew nothing would ever, ever be the same again.

He grinned, remembering everything, every perfect, miraculous moment, every kiss and touch and sigh. He glanced up again at the goddesses, and they seemed to smile down at him in return. Even they were happy for him now.

May had truly brought springtime into his life at last.

He shifted and found he laid on one of the white satin settees, a fur-lined blanket tucked softly around him. And May, wonderful, perfect, darling May, slept against his chest, her arms wrapped around him, her waves of red-gold hair binding them together, the bodice of her gown loosened where he'd kissed her creamy shoulders.

Connor smiled and drew her even closer, that lilac perfume tickling delightfully at his nose. It was exactly as he had dreamed. May with him, exhausted, the cold house touched at last with the warmth of real life. He kissed her bare shoulder, every tiny pale freckle dotted there.

She stirred and stretched, her eyes fluttering open to gaze up at him. For a moment, a lazy, slow, gratifyingly satisfied smile spread over her lips, dark pink from his kisses. "Connor," she whispered, then she froze. She shot straight up, tugging the blanket with her, much to his disappointment.

"What time is it?" she gasped. "Is it morning?"

He sat up beside her and pressed another kiss to her bare shoulder, savoring the taste of her. The scent of her. "Not yet morning, don't worry."

"Don't worry?" she whispered. She glanced around frantically for her clothes, her fine gown and gossamer underthings scattered over the carpet, her stockings caught on one of the Venetian chandeliers, her hairpins everywhere. "My parents..."

"I will have you home in plenty of time. And somehow, I don't think they will mind so very much." He reached for his crumpled evening coat, balled up on the floor under the settee, and took out the velvet box to flip it open. The faint candlelight from one of the sputtering candelabras caught on the pale blue aquamarine, sparkling like a star, casting a celestial glow all its own. He had taken back the first, large ring and found this one instead, a dainty, pretty jewel that reminded him of May. Of springtime skies.

May's hand flew to her lips as she gaped at it. "Is that..."

"It is yours, if you'll take it." He took it from the box and held it out to her, his heart pounding with fear and hope all at once. "My heart and soul, all I have and will ever have, I'm offering to you. I love you, May. I can't imagine my life without you. I know I was a fool at first, a looby who had no idea how to win a lady as wonderful as you. But I've loved you since the moment I saw you, and I always will."

"Oh, Connor," she murmured, her eyes bright with tears.

"And if you don't like this house, it's too big or too small, we'll knock it down and start again," he hurried onward, afraid she would say no. If she did, then all was ruined. "Or build something else entirely, someplace else! Do you like Paris? Or somewhere warm? Hawaii, maybe? It is all yours. Jewels, gowns, carriages…"

"Connor!" she said, laughing. She reached out and caught his face between her hands, her expression glowing with a joy that echoed his own. "I want none of those things. I would live in a tree house in the woods if I can just be with you. I love you, too."

"You—love me?" He could hardly dare believe she had just said that, that she loved *him*, a boyo from the Lower East Side.

"How could I not? You are so kind, so funny and, yes, so very handsome. So I will marry you. Yes."

Connor trembled as he slipped the ring onto May's finger.

She leaned against him with the happiest of sighs. "Perfect. Just what I would have chosen myself. Oh, Connor. How did I get so very lucky?"

Her laughed. "You'll be an O'Neill now, my love.

That means you'll have the luck of the Irish with you all the time. Just as I have right now, with you, my perfect springtime May."

Epilogue

The *New York World* newspaper Society column

Such an event has, this writer dares to say, never been seen in New York before! The O'Neill Christmas ball is the *soiree of the festive season, and we hold our breath to see who has received one of the rumored thirteen hundred invitations.*

Oh, for a glimpse of that palace on Fifth Avenue, hitherto hidden from sight! There shall be two orchestras, a midnight supper catered by Delmonico's. Klanders florist is quite emptied of blooms; couturiers, milliners, chefs, jewelers... all slaving for weeks.

Nobody has yet seen the lair of the Wizard of Railroads. Will it live up to all expectations? And will an anticipated announcement concerning a certain Miss VDB take place?

We are all agog.

At the Christmas ball

May stood by the window of the guest chamber where she prepared for the ball, watching the scene outside as Rose fluttered around putting the final touches on her attire. May had never seen anything quite like it all before, and it made such butterflies of fear and excitement and joy tremble in her stomach.

Was she ready for this life, so different from what she'd always known?

When she lay in Connor's arms, nothing else mattered. She was sure she could do anything at all! Now, as she watched the crowds outside on the snowy walkway, held back by rows of police, saw the footmen clad in dark blue silk knee breeches and powdered wigs roll out a matching gold-edged blue carpet from the awning over the doors down the steps to the edge of the street, she didn't know.

This would be her life now, queen of this palace. It was rather terrifying. But then she thought of Connor, his teasing smiles, the touch of his hand, and she knew he was all that was important. All she wanted.

As Rose fastened May's gown, the most beautiful thing she'd ever known, rose-pink and cloud-white from Worth, with antique lace and pearl-encrusted lilies of the valley, darkness fell outside. But around Connor's house, it was like noontime, shining with light at every window, festive with wreaths and bows and streamers.

By ten o'clock, gleaming carriages arrived, and their occupants stepped down directly onto the carpet, wrapped in furs and velvet. They hurried up the steps, the crowds shouting after the most popular beauties, the most hated robber barons, and May knew she would soon have to make her own appearance.

She turned to examine herself in the full-length mirror, and for a moment she didn't quite know herself at all. Who was this vision of pink and white, a pearl collar at her throat, her hair piled high and crowned with a pearl-and-diamond tiara?

But there was no time to hesitate. The shouts from outside grew louder, and Rose said, "Are you ready, then, Miss May?"

May drew in a deep breath and clasped her gloved hands together to keep from shaking. "Yes, indeed." She half wanted to hide under the bed. But only if Connor was there with her, and he waited downstairs.

Rose handed her the spangled lace fan, straightened the pearl-edged train, and May marched out of the chamber.

She paused to examine the dining room where the buffet supper was being laid, the ballroom where the musicians played, the small sitting rooms set up for quiet chats. It was all transformed from the cold, empty place she had first seen, and it sparkled and dazzled, just as Connor's house should. The florists had done their very best, festooning the rooms with large wreaths of greenery and red roses, palm fronds towering in silver pots in the corners, vases of American Beauty and Jacqueminot roses, Malmaison carnations, red and white and pink.

Entire trees had been brought in, too, none as towering as the Christmas tree itself but all sparkling with lights. The air smelled of the flowers, sweet and heady, mixed with the spices of the Christmas punch and the ladies' French perfumes, the smoke from the thousands of candles and the Yule logs in the fireplaces.

May took her place on the first staircase landing with her parents, Mrs. O'Neill and Jane, where they would greet their guests. Connor hadn't appeared yet, and May felt a pang of worry. What if he did *not* appear? What if all this, all this joy and hope, was for nothing?

She glanced down at her finger, where the ring sat beneath her glove, waiting to be revealed.

"Do cease fidgeting, May," her mother chided. "It's a ball! Look happy, my dearest."

"I am happy, Mama," May said, and she truly was, despite her worries. She smiled at her mother.

Adelaide looked lovely, in a new gown of peacock-blue satin and velvet. The worry lines on her face had faded, and her eyes glowed with triumph. She reached out for Henry's arm to stop him fidgeting; it had been so hard to drag him from the library.

Jane grinned at May, and even Mrs. O'Neill looked happy. This was their home, too, their triumph.

And at last Connor came dashing down the stairs, still smoothing his hair and straightening his white evening tie, pinned with a sapphire to match the edges of May's new ring.

"Forgive my tardiness," he said, bowing over Adelaide's hand, kissing his mother's cheek, then bending over May's hand with a teasing grin. "I had a gift I had to fetch from the safe."

"Oh, Connor!" his mother chided. "We agreed, no gifts until Twelfth Night."

"But May should have this for tonight." He handed her the small package, watched closely as she unwrapped it. Inside was another ring, not like her aquamarine engagement ring but a small gold circlet shaped into a pair of clasped hands over a heart. It was plain, a bit battered and entirely beautiful. "It was my father's mother's, in Ireland. It will bring you the luck of the O'Neills."

"It is the loveliest thing ever," she whispered, and clutched it close as if it could send that luck straight inside of her now, and for the rest of the evening. The rest of their lives together.

She couldn't say anything else, for the front doors opened in the foyer below on the chime of ten o'clock. The maids and footmen below took their fur-trimmed wraps, and Makepeace, the butler, led them up the staircase, a kaleidoscope of satins and silks and tulles, a tangle of laughter and awed glances.

And the jewels! They alone made day into night. Fringe tiaras, diamond stars, necklaces of rubies and emeralds and amethysts, pearl dog collars as Princess Alexandra wore, bow brooches, lover's knot buttons. Grandest of all was *the* Mrs. Astor herself, who swept up the stairs with her friend, the stout, mustachioed Ward McAllister and her daughter Carrie, her famous diamond stomacher blazing on her black velvet gown.

"Mrs. O'Neill," she said, barely offering her gloved fingertips. It was like a royal benediction. "What elegant arrangements. Thank you for your kind invitation. Mr. and Mrs. Van Der Berg, how nice to see you again." And that was it. She continued up the stairs to the ballroom.

"That is *it*, Ma!" Jane whispered excitedly. "We are accepted now."

"Thanks to my beautiful bride," Connor whispered in May's ear, taking the chance to press a wanton kiss to her throat. May giggled. Not even Mrs. Astor could compare to such joy.

After the last of the guests were admitted, May took Connor's offered arm and followed her parents into the ballroom, fairly dancing already. "No escape now," she whispered to him as she took in the transformed space. The enormous tree, the lights, the flowers, the lilting music, the snow starting to fall beyond the windows, it was like a dream.

"Do you want to escape?" he whispered back. "There's a back door."

"I am sure there are many. But now that I have you, I won't let you go." She laughed to think of all the elopements she'd read about in novels, two lovers dashing alone into the night, and for an instant she was tempted.

"Perhaps we really should have eloped," she mused. "You, me, a vicar, and we would be wed. We could do…" She went up on tiptoe and whispered in his ear some of the naughty things she would much like to try, now that she knew how delightful lovemaking could really be. She laughed when a dusky pink actually touched his cheekbones.

"Let's go, then," he said, and tugged at her arm.

May laughed even harder. "And disappoint our mothers so? They've been staying up nights going over ribbons and roses and lace. Before Lent will be soon enough—I hope."

He looked rather disgruntled. "Humph. If you say so."

"It is our duty. And we haven't even announced it yet."

The musicians in the gallery launched into a Lehár piece, and the dancers for the first quadrille, the Mythology Quadrille, swept out onto the parquet floor, their draped, pale classical gowns swirling, arms fluttering. Jane was in the midst of them all, every eligible young man vying to partner her.

May and Connor took their blue velvet seats on a dais with their parents, watching as the dancers made their way through the intricate steps and patterns, though May had to admit she really only saw, only knew, Connor, sitting there so close to her. As he always would be.

At last, the set ended, and before the opening mazurka began, May's father rose to his feet.

"Our dear friends," he said slowly, as if making speeches was something he hadn't done in a very long while. May suspected never. "I am so pleased to announce the betrothal of our only child, Miss May Van Der Berg, to Mr. Connor O'Neill, and wish them every happiness in their lives ahead." He kissed May's cheek as Adelaide sniffled and Connor's mother passed her a handkerchief.

Connor held out his hand to May, and together they stepped to the edge of the dais. Applause rippled through the room as Connor ducked his head and kissed her, softly at first, gently, then deeper, hotter, a kiss to seal their love for all time, in front of the whole world.

"This is forever, isn't it?" he murmured, staring deep into her eyes.

May smiled, so filled with the golden glow of happiness she was sure she would burst with it. "Oh, yes, Connor, my darling. Forever and ever, always."

* * * * *

Author Note

〜〜〜

> *"We have no right to exclude those whom the growth of this great country has brought forward, provided they are not vulgar in speech and appearance. The time has come for the Vanderbilts."*

> The Mrs. Astor

When I was asked about writing a Gilded Age novella I was so excited! I might even have done a few jumpy claps. Especially after writing my Victorian *Dollar Duchesses* trilogy, about three New York heiresses marrying English dukes.

I had been wanting so much to revisit the era. I've been obsessed with it ever since first reading Edith Wharton's novels as a teenager. *The Age of Innocence* is a favorite book, and I always wondered what it would have been like with a happier ending…

The great changes, the contrasts, the architecture

and fashion, the larger-than-life historical figures—all so fascinating. And I found so much inspiration for Connor and May's story in those real-life Gilded Age people!

The early eighteen-eighties were especially ripe for social change. The queen bee of New York society for many years had been The Knickerbocker, Mrs. Caroline Schermerhorn Astor, known as "The Mrs. Astor." Upholders of old money and tradition, Astor and Ward McAllister, the self-appointed "arbiter of social taste" and creator of the Four Hundred—supposedly how many people would fit in the Astor ballroom—were the gatekeepers of all things upper-class. It was up to them to decide if your bloodlines were pure enough or your last name respectable enough to become one of the elite.

Until along came Alva Vanderbilt. Daughter of an old but impoverished family, and wife of William K. Vanderbilt, one of the richest men in New York, she couldn't quite crack the Four Hundred, despite her cultured good taste and fierce energy. So she started her siege by commissioning Richard Morris Hunt to build her a "Petit Chateau" at 660 Fifth Avenue—a vast, elaborate palace that she filled with art and antiques. Then she was ready to throw the biggest house-warming party ever, on March 26, 1883.

Uniformed servants hand-delivered invitations,

young socialites practiced quadrilles for weeks—dances performed with four couples in a rectangular formation—and, according to the *New York Times*, "Amid the rush and excitement of business, men find their minds haunted by uncontrollable thoughts as to whether they should appear as Robert Le Diable, Cardinal Richelieu, Otho the Barbarian, or the Count of Monte Cristo, while the ladies are driven to the verge of distraction in an effort to settle the comparative advantages of ancient, medieval, and modern costumes."

According to gossip, Alva employed good old-fashioned manipulation, and used Mrs. Astor's daughter, Carrie, as a pawn. Like all young women of marrying age, Carrie had practiced a quadrille with her friends for weeks, and anxiously awaited her invitation. When all her friends had got theirs, and she still hadn't, she asked her mother to find out why.

Alva claimed that since Mrs. Astor had never called on the Vanderbilt home on Fifth Avenue to introduce herself formally, she had no address to send an invitation, so Mrs. Astor reluctantly visited Petit Chateau and left her visiting card. Their invitation was received the following day.

Some twelve hundred New York socialites began arriving in carriages at the mansion at ten p.m. as the fancy dress ball got underway. Police had to hold back the crowds gathered to catch a glimpse of the society "it" men and women in their creative and over-the-top costumes.

Mrs. Astor and Ward McAllister attended, and hundreds of other costumed guests drank champagne and danced around the flower-filled house and the third-floor gymnasium, which had been converted into a forest filled with orchids, bougainvillea and palm trees.

A small staff of servants served dinner at two a.m., including chicken croquettes, Maryland-style terrapin, fried oysters, beef, ham and chicken in jelly, salmon *à la* Rothschild, chicken salad *au celery*, sandwiches *à la* Windsor, and several kinds of ices.

The dancing continued until sunrise, when Alva led her guests in a final Virginia reel.

Most contemporary sources put the cost of the ball at two hundred and fifty thousand dollars—around six million in today's money—including sixty-five thousand dollars for champagne and eleven thousand dollars for flowers.

The story May tells Connor about the New Year's Eve reception, with the young man relieving himself in the fireplace, is also bizarrely true!

The New Year's reception was a tradition among old New York families—like the Archers and the Wellands in *The Age of Innocence*—and gentlemen would go from house to house among their acquaintance to pay calls, take refreshments and court eligible young ladies.

A man named James Gordon Bennett, scion of a well-known family and famous as a rake, who loved practical jokes—his favorite hobby was riding his horse naked at midnight—became engaged to a respectable young lady named Caroline May. He arrived drunk at her parents' New Year's reception, staggered into the drawing room, unfastened his trousers, and relieved himself on the fire.

Women screamed, Caroline fled in tears, and her brothers threw him out in the snow and beat him up the next day at their club. The engagement was certainly off!

Connor, of course, would never, *ever* behave that way to our May!

I hope you have enjoyed their story as much as I loved writing it.

Here are few fun sources for the period:

King, Greg (2009) *A Season of Splendor: The Court of Mrs. Astor in Gilded Age New York*. Wiley

Vanderbilt Balsan, Consuelo (1953) *The Glitter and the Gold*. St. Martin's Press

Barrault, Jean-Michel (2004) *Yachting: The Golden Age*. Hachette UK

Benway, Ann (1984) *A Guide to Newport Mansions*. The Preservation Society of Newport County

Coleman, Elizabeth Ann (1989) *The Opulent Era: Fashion of Worth, Doucet, and Pingat*. Thames & Hudson

Rugoff, Milton (1989) *America's Gilded Age*. Henry Holt & Co

Tichi, Cecelia (2018) *What Would Mrs. Astor Do?* NYU Press

THE RAILROAD BARON'S MISTLETOE BRIDE

Lauri Robinson

Dedicated to Jessica, an amazing young woman
who I have the honor of calling my niece.

Chapter One

Chilled to the bone, Kurt Cavanaugh straightened his overcoat as he climbed out of the stage. Tiny, barely visible bits of snow were being whipped around with the force of a blizzard behind them. They only increased his frustration. He'd never failed at completing tasks asked of him on behalf of his family and the East Central Railroad, with pride and determination to keep the East Central the top railroad in the nation, but this task angered him.

The fact that his grandfather had withheld the information that his brother had fathered a child years ago was not only a betrayal, it was cruel.

Cruel to the child and the child's mother.

Cruel to him for having to face Harper Hollister under such circumstances.

Cruel to her for having to raise her niece.

Just cruel all the way around.

If only he'd known sooner, he could have done

something to help her. He hadn't known, not until listening to his grandfather's sincerely apologetic confession and plea to meet his only great-grandchild.

Kurt wasn't here just for his grandfather's benefit. The child was a Cavanaugh and deserved the benefits of that.

Pine City, located in a rural area of Pennsylvania, was small and, from the looks of it, hadn't advanced much since its incorporation, which, in his opinion, appeared to have happened decades ago.

Kurt stretched out the kinks in his arms and legs from being cooped up in the cold stagecoach for the last three hours, then walked forward and stepped up onto the wooden walkway beneath the overhang that ran the length of the wooden buildings lining the street. He was no stranger to traveling, but normally did so in the comfort of a train, in one of his personal Pullman cars.

There wasn't a depot in Pine City, nor tracks nearby. The closest depot was twenty miles away, hence the reason he'd traveled by stage for this leg of his trip.

"Your bag, sir," the stagecoach driver said.

Kurt reached up and took the leather bag the man held over the edge of the coach. "Thank you. What time does the stage depart town tomorrow?"

"Same as today. Four o'clock," the driver responded. "You can buy tickets just up the street at Johnson's Department Store."

"Thank you." Johnson's Department Store was also where he'd find Harper Hollister. She worked there. The Pinkerton agent he'd hired had provided him with all of the information he needed to find his niece.

Kurt looked up and down the street at the various weatherworn buildings as he asked, "Do you know if this town has a hotel?"

Still sitting in the driver's seat, the grizzled old driver pointed in the same direction as a moment ago. "Up the street, next door to Johnson's Department Store is the Johnson Hotel."

Kurt gave a nod of courtesy. "Very well, thank you."

"Hi, Mr. Duncan!" a little voice shouted.

The driver's grin showed he only had a few teeth left, but his face lit up like a boy's. "Well, if'n it ain't my favorite person in all of Pennsylvania. How are you today, Miss Katie Jo?"

"I'm happy!" A young girl, bundled in a red coat and wearing a red knit hat, ran up the boardwalk with long braids flapping against her shoulders. She waved a sheet of paper. "I got an A on my spelling test!"

Kurt grinned. She was missing her two front top teeth. Then he noticed her eyes and his grin faded.

Big, round and thickly lashed, her eyes were a unique shade of blue.

"Of course, you did!" the driver replied. "You must be the smartest girl in the whole town, mayhap the state, if not the entire nation."

"Want to see it?" she asked, her eyes beaming as she arrived next to the stage.

"I do." The driver looked at him. "Mister, would you mind handing me up Miss Katie Jo's test? If'n I get down, I'll have a hard time getting back up here."

"Of course." Kurt took the paper the girl eagerly held out to him and handed it up to the driver. With her chubby face, rosy cheeks and button nose dotted with freckles, the girl could be on a Christmas card. The missing front teeth only added to her cherub appearance.

"Well, now, lookie here," the driver exclaimed. "There's a big red A printed at the top. That's mighty fine spelling, Miss Katie."

"Thank you, Mr. Duncan." Her expression grew serious as she turned those blue eyes Kurt's way while saying, "I'll be needing that back, Mister, to show my sister."

"Yes, you will." Kurt took note of the word *sister* as he retrieved the piece of paper from the driver. "May I look at it first?"

"Sure." Her head bobbed and pride made her stand a bit taller.

Kurt was impressed by both the penmanship and the correct spelling of ten four- and five-letter words and made a point of showing that by letting out a low whistle. "This certainly is impressive. Those are some difficult words."

"Thank you. I am an exceptional speller," she said, with no qualms about being boastful.

The missing teeth gave her a slight lisp that was nearly as charming as her personality. "I see you are." He'd also noticed the name printed at the top of the sheet. "And your name is Katherine."

"Yes, sir," she replied. "That's what the teacher calls me, but everyone else calls me Katie Jo."

The report he'd received from the detective said his niece's name was Katherine, and Kurt highly doubted that Pine City was large enough to have two six-year-olds with that name. He was guessing at her age, but not her eyes. Those were Cavanaugh blue eyes. He saw the shade, halfway between green and blue, every time he looked in the mirror. His brother Kent had those same eyes. As had his father. His grandfather insisted they'd all inherited them from his late wife, their grandmother Victoria.

He handed the paper back to her and held out his other hand in offer of a handshake. "Hello, Katie

Jo, my name is Kurt. It's very nice to make your acquaintance."

She eyed him with a slight frown. "Are you a salesman?"

"No, I am not." Curious, he asked, "Why?"

"Because I'm not allowed to talk to salesmen," she said quite seriously. "That's Mr. Johnson's job."

He nodded, as if that was all the explanation he needed. "I see. Well, then it's a good thing that I'm not a salesman. However..." He paused and glanced up the street. "I am on my way to Johnson's Department Store. Perhaps you could show me the way?"

"I can do that!" Her frown fully disappeared. "That's where I work."

"Work?"

"Yes, sir." She took hold of his hand and gave a solid attempt at pumping it in a handshake. "It's nice to meet you, too." She waved at the driver. "Bye, Mr. Duncan. See you tomorrow!"

"I'll be right here," the driver answered as he took a bag from a man ready to board the stage.

Kurt assumed the man would be the only passenger, as he had been.

Katie Jo took hold of his hand again and gave it a little tug. "I'm not supposed to dawdle on my way home."

Kurt fell in step beside her and, noting how chilly

her small fingers felt against his palm, he folded his fingers tighter around her hand to warm it. "I believe you need a pair of mittens."

"Oh!" She pulled her hand out of his and quickly dug a pair of red mittens out of her pocket. "I forgot to put them on."

"Here, I'll hold your test for you."

She handed over the prized sheet of paper and once the mittens were in place, she took the test back and grasped his hand again. "Harper says I don't want to catch a cold before Christmas. We have too much to do."

He'd just received confirmation of her identity. "Oh, what is it that you have to do?"

"We have to get a Christmas tree and string popcorn and make ornaments, bake sugar cookies with Mrs. Johnson and wrap the present I made for Mrs. Crumb and..." She continued to name off tasks as they walked along the boardwalk, occasionally explaining who some of the people were that she mentioned, including Mrs. Crumb, who always looks grumpy, but that's because her husband died and she lives all by herself now.

Kurt nodded in agreement when she looked up at him but, for the most part, simply walked along beside her, listening as she talked. However, his mind was more on her aunt, Harper. He was certain that she was not going to be as welcoming to him as Katie Jo.

"Uh-oh," Katie Jo said, cutting herself off in the middle of talking about gingerbread houses.

Kurt's gaze followed in the direction of Katie Jo's, and his breath caught at the sight of the woman hurrying out of a door and then coming to a stop on the boardwalk. Slim, yet shapely, Harper Hollister hadn't changed in the past seven years. She was still the prettiest woman he'd ever laid eyes on. Her brown hair was pinned back in a way that made it puff out around her slender face, much like when she used to work at the train station, and she still had the same big brown eyes that he'd admired.

However, the expression on that lovely face said she recognized him, and she was not happy.

If he had to guess, he'd say she was borderline furious.

Harper Hollister felt as if the world had stopped turning. Either that, or it had spun so fast and hard that it had thrown her into her worst nightmare. Kurt Cavanaugh had found her. Somewhere deep inside, she'd known that a Cavanaugh would find her and Katie Jo eventually. She had expected it to be Kent.

The Cavanaugh family had the money to find anyone, anywhere. She'd hoped that they wouldn't care enough to look for her, because that was the other thing they had plenty of—disinterest in anyone but themselves. The only thing they cared about was money. They were Baltimore blue bloods, amassing more wealth for their old money coffers was their ultimate goal.

Baltimore was known as the birthplace of the railroad due to the Cavanaughs. They'd pioneered the first railroad in America right there in Baltimore in the early eighteen hundreds and had since grown it into the largest one in the nation—and they weren't done. They continued to lay tracks, add locomotives and line their pockets.

Every part of her being was trembling, and Harper had no idea what to do, other than to get Katie Jo as far away from Kurt as possible. From any Cavanaugh. That had been her goal since the moment her niece had been born.

"Katie Jo. Inside. Now," she said sternly, lifting a shaking hand to point toward the doorway of the store that she'd exited.

"I remembered my mittens and my hat, Harper," Katie Jo said. "And I got an A on my test."

Harper fully knew it was unfair to take any of her distress out in the form of anger toward Katie Jo, but the fear of what Kurt could do overrode everything else.

He leaned down slightly and said something to Katie Jo, who nodded and scurried forward.

"He's not a salesman," Katie Jo said, while scampering past and into the store.

Harper pinched her lips together. She knew exactly who he was.

Broad shouldered and tall, with light brown hair and the same shade of blue-green eyes that Katie Jo had, Kurt Cavanaugh was the first and, truly, the only man who had ever made her heart beat too fast and her palms sweat. Both of those things were happening now.

However, this time, those reactions were caused by fear.

"Hello, Miss Hollister," he said, keeping his eyes locked with hers.

She pressed her toes firmly against the boardwalk to keep herself from turning about and running. She couldn't escape him. Facing him was her only option.

"Or perhaps I'm incorrect. It's been years. Is it Mrs....?"

Her mouth was so dry her tongue didn't want to work. She licked at her lips, hoping that would help, and tried again. "No."

He gave a nod, as if her answer somehow pleased him, or perhaps he'd already known. Most likely he had. The fact that he was here meant that he knew all there was to know about her and Katie Jo. Or so he thought, because he was probably under the impression that it would be easy to take Katie Jo away from her. It wouldn't be.

"I imagine you know why I'm here," he said.

There was no denying he'd discovered the truth, and her heart sank all the way to her toes. Forcing herself not to let any sign of the chaos that was happening inside her show, she stood stock-still and kept her gaze locked with his.

"Is there someplace we could talk in private?" he asked.

"No!" She clamped her lips together long enough to gather her wits. Or at least attempt to. "I'm working."

"What time are you done?" he asked.

Before she could answer, he noticed the sign in the window. The one that held both the time the store opened and the time that it closed.

"Five o'clock," he said. "That will give me time to check into the hotel."

Her entire world was falling apart, and she cursed herself for not preparing for this moment. "Katie Jo doesn't know," she said quietly.

"I assumed as much when she referred to you as her sister," Kurt answered. "It would be best if you and I spoke in private. Will that be possible at five o'clock?"

Would this be easier if he was mad, yelling at her that he knew Katie Jo was his brother's child? She doubted it, but he was being so calm, so unruffled. Then again, he'd always been kind and courteous. All of the waitresses had rushed to be the one to wait on him when he'd entered the train depot restaurant years ago. They'd done the same for his brother, Kent. She'd never been one of those girls. She'd been there to work, earn enough money to feed her family and nothing more. If only Sherri had been, too.

If only she'd discovered how ruthless the Cavanaughs were then. But that would have meant Katie Jo never being born, and that would have been tragic. Katie Jo had been a bright spot in the world since the moment she'd been born.

"Harper," he said quietly and then corrected himself. "Miss Hollister, I understand my arrival is a shock. It would be best for us to discuss it in private, not the middle of the boardwalk."

She nodded, only because he was right.

"Would you be willing to come to the hotel after you're finished working?" he asked. "If not, I could come to your residence."

She could only imagine how that would look to the town. It was a horse apiece. Either option was going to cause gossip. So was standing in the middle of the street. "I'll come to the hotel."

"Thank you." He glanced over her shoulder to the hotel next door. "I'll meet you in the lobby shortly after five."

Chapter Two

Harper did her best to pretend that nothing was amiss when she entered the store, going straight to the newly arrived selection of toys that she'd been putting in the window display when she'd seen Katie Jo through the glass, walking with a man. She was still shaking. Even after all these years, she had recognized Kurt immediately.

Elanor Johnson, who was as dear as the day was long, and had eyes in the back of her head, arrived at her side before Harper had been able to take a full breath. Her chest was still too constricted for that to happen.

"Is everything all right, dear?"

The concern in Elanor's voice was almost enough to break Harper. She was grateful for both Elanor and her husband, Wayne Johnson. They'd been so good to her and Katie Jo from the moment they'd arrived in Pine City, practically penniless and Katie Jo a tiny infant. "Yes," she answered.

Nobody's fool, Elanor leaned over so they were face to face and looked over the top rim of her glasses. "Is he an old friend?"

Elanor's question was barely a whisper, and Harper was thankful that her answer wasn't a lie. "No." She sucked in the deep breath that she'd been needing and continued, "But I do need to speak with him after we close. Could Katie Jo stay with you for a short time?"

"Most certainly. I've promised her that we'll make sugar cookies, so you take your time."

Having only one child, an unmarried son, Leonard, who managed the hotel next door, Elanor had appointed herself as a grandmother figure to Katie Jo and played the role to its finest. Harper would forever be grateful to Elanor for all she did for them, though she did her best not to take advantage of anyone's kindness. "Thank you," she said. "I will be next door, at the hotel, and won't be gone long."

"You can eat there, save yourself from cooking," Elanor said. "Katie Jo will eat with me and Wayne."

"That's not necessary. I won't be gone that long." There was no way on earth that she would turn Katie Jo over to the Cavanaughs, and it wouldn't take her long to let Kurt know that.

At five o'clock, Harper didn't bother checking her reflection in a mirror, nor did she take the time to collect her coat from the back room. She merely took off her white, pocketed apron, hung it behind the counter and exited through the front door to walk the short distance to the hotel. There wasn't a single part of her that wasn't shaking, trembling, and she kept one hand pressed against her churning stomach.

The churning increased when the hotel door opened, and it was Kurt. Dressed in his tailored brown suit, shined shoes and pressed white shirt, he looked as dandy as a day, and as out of place in Pine City as a man could get. His kind was never out of place in Baltimore. There, blue blood families, dressed in all their finery, boast that there are more millionaire philanthropists in their city than any other in America. They boast about donations to the libraries, the parks, the hospitals and other noble causes, but never once do they say that the money donated was made off the backs of the people who work in the factories, the railyards and the shipyards, day in and day out, barely making enough money to feed their families.

She knew. Her father had been one of those workers and had lost his life working for the East Central Railroad, but nobody had cared about that. Nobody had cared that his death had left two young girls—she'd been seventeen and Sherri sixteen—to fend for themselves. To give up their dreams and take jobs at the railroad-owned restaurant in order to pay rent on the company-owned house they had lived in nearly their entire lives.

She would never be trapped like that again, nor would she allow that to happen to Katie Jo.

"Miss Hollister," Kurt said, holding the door open.

Head up, Harper stepped over the threshold, and when he placed a hand on the small of her back, she jolted forward, spun around and shot him a glare.

"Forgive me," he said quietly. "I was merely going to steer you toward the hotel office, not the dining room." He gestured toward the desk near the stairway. "Mr. Johnson has provided us the use of his office so we'll have privacy."

She should be grateful for that, but currently, the best she could do was breathe through her fear and anger, and how her back felt as if it was on fire. He kept his hand to himself as she walked around the desk and then through the door that was open several feet behind it.

The room, with one wall of shelves that held extra linens and supplies, the small wooden table and chairs, the filing cabinet and the mirrored buffet that had been moved from the dining room when they'd added more seating room, was all familiar to her. She'd worked at the hotel before the department store and still helped out at the hotel when needed.

"Please," Kurt said, pointing to one of the two chairs flanking the table, while closing the door.

Although she'd prefer to stand, Harper didn't trust her legs. She sat and ran her hands over her skirt. Her palms were sweating. Arriving at this hotel years ago had been such a relief on that cold and snowy night. Her plan had been to continue north, but by the time the weather had cleared, she'd concluded that Pine City had everything that she'd been looking for—no train station and no chance of one being built. Without either of those things, there was no reason for a Cavanaugh to ever enter the town. So, she'd stayed.

It had worked perfectly for almost seven years. Elanor and Wayne had been running both the store and the hotel then, with Leonard's help, but he'd only been seventeen and hadn't taken over the hotel until four years later, when Elanor thought him an appropriate age.

The stagecoach wheels had been so coated in snow they could barely turn that February evening, and Katie Jo had only been two weeks old. With exactly ten dollars and sixty-seven cents to her name, after paying for Sherri's funeral, the doctor for delivering Katie Jo and for their travels, Harper had checked in to the hotel and asked if she could purchase a can of evaporated milk for Katie Jo. Almost instantly, Elanor provided one and settled them into a hotel room. The only move they'd made since then was to the apartment above the store when Leonard had moved into the hotel, and Elanor and Wayne had moved into the house behind the store, where Wayne's mother had lived until last year when she'd passed away. Bless her soul.

"I would like to begin by offering my condolences for the loss of your sister," Kurt said, sitting down across from her. "It's my understanding that she passed away giving birth to Katie Jo."

Harper wanted to correct him, tell him that her niece's name was Katherine, but that was a moot point. It was just that she wanted to protect Katie Jo from him and his family. She wasn't prepared for this, but told herself that she needed to acknowledge his condolences, for whatever they were worth. "Thank you." She swallowed. "Yes, she did."

"May I also apologize for you having to bear the burden of raising our niece on your own for the past six, almost seven, years."

It took Harper a moment to pull apart her lips, which she'd needed to bite together to keep from saying that Katie Jo was her niece, not his. But she *was* his niece, too. However, she couldn't stifle her response to the rest of his statement. "Katie Jo is not a burden. She never has been and never will be."

"Forgive me, but you misunderstood. I did not say she was a burden. I apologized for you carrying the burden of raising her on your own. Had you contacted me, I—"

"Why would I have contacted you?"

"...would have shared the burden with you," he continued, as if she hadn't interrupted him.

She would never have contacted him or his brother, because they would have taken Katie Jo away from her. She might not have the money he did, but she was no longer the young girl who used to wait tables. She'd matured, and would not be intimidated by him. "Why would you share the burden with me? She's not your child. She's your brother's child." Tears stung her eyes. She blinked and looked away, trying to stop them. Just saying that aloud reinforced the fact that Katie Jo didn't belong to her. "He's the one I thought would track us down. Attempt to take her away from me." Anger rose again. "But evidently, his daughter means no more to him than my sister had."

"You don't know, do you?"

"That he's married?" Lifting her chin, she met his gaze. "Yes. I know that he's married. I also know that he promised to marry my sister. To give her the life she could only dream of, but he didn't do that. He left her unwed and pregnant, while he married someone else." A blue blood, that's who he'd married, because that's what blue bloods do. The anger at Kent that she'd kept bottled up, anger for the pain and suffering he'd put Sherri through, was bursting to get out. He was the reason her sister had died. Heartbroken when she heard he'd gotten married, Sherri had cried for weeks on end and hadn't had the will to do anything. By the time she'd given birth, she'd been so weak, so frail, there hadn't been anything the doctor could do to save her.

Harper jumped to her feet, slammed her hands on the table. "He abandoned his daughter before she was even born, and I refuse to allow him to disrupt her life now! I am the only family Katie Jo knows!"

The Pinkerton agent had been very thorough, and though Kurt knew that Harper and Katie Jo had lived in Pine City since shortly after Sherri Hollister had died, he could only imagine the anguish that Harper had gone through. He could understand her anger.

He could also understand her fear.

Reaching across the table, he touched the back of her hand with four fingers. "Kent is dead, Harper."

Her eyes grew wide, and for several still moments, she stared at him, somewhat blankly, then slowly lowered onto her chair. "Dead?"

"Yes," he replied. The loss of his only sibling, his brother, was still inside him, would always be inside, but he'd come to terms with it. Accepted it, because life does go on. He thought it was all behind him, the tragedy and loss. Until his grandfather had told him about Katie Jo. That had added to the pain of what could have been. Should have been, but wasn't. "Kent and his wife, Alice, died in a hotel fire while on their honeymoon in Europe."

Harper let out a soft, emotion-filled gasp and laid her other hand atop his. "I'm sorry, I—I hadn't heard that. Hadn't known. I am very sorry for your loss."

Her sincerity touched him. Even with her own fears and pain laid bare, she had the wherewithal to feel sorrow for others. That was testament to her character. He'd always known she had integrity. That's what had drawn him to her years ago. Her authenticity.

He laid his free hand over the top of hers, making a stack out of their hands. "I believe there are a lot of things neither of us knew, Harper. That's why I'm here."

Her brown eyes were full of expression. Sympathy and sorrow were there. So was skepticism.

He wrapped his fingers around the backs of her hands in a gentle squeeze. The frustration he'd felt since learning about Katie Jo's existence peaked again. The entire affair had been cruel and had affected so many lives. He would do what had to be done, while making sure that neither Harper nor

Katie Jo were harmed in any way. "I'm not here to take Katie Jo away from you, Harper."

She swallowed visibly and stared harder, as if she was searching for a sign to tell her if he was telling the truth or not.

"Then why are you here?" she asked. "There's nothing in Pine City for you."

"You are here," he said, "and Katie Jo."

She waited for him to say more. Expectancy was on her face, in those big brown eyes. He'd thought of those eyes over the years. She hadn't been like the other waitresses at the train station near the Delaware border, who had known who he was and had rushed to serve him, flirted, made propositions. He'd been used to that even way back then, knew how to deflect their advances without hurting their feelings. He hadn't had to do that with her. She'd simply been honestly friendly and adorably secretive in telling him what not to order. That had become a game they'd played, and he'd looked forward to scanning the menu and watching her shake her head or nod, with a bright smile on her face.

At the time, he hadn't known Sherri was her sister, hadn't known Sherri at all. All he'd known was that one day, Harper was no longer working at the restaurant. That had been shortly after Kent's death, and for some reason, he'd really wanted to see her that day.

He'd only known her first name from the tag she'd worn on her blue uniform and had stopped eating there after she left. Yet, he'd thought about her for years, had wondered what had happened to her. He'd eventually concluded that she'd married, and that some man was extremely lucky to be her husband.

Slowly, she pulled her hands out of the stack and lowered them onto her lap beneath the table.

His hands had never felt so empty. He leaned back in his chair. "I'm not sure where to start," he said, for that was the truth. "Other than to promise you, a very solemn promise, that I will not take Katie Jo away from you."

Her eyes narrowed, once again filled with suspicion.

"I could. I have the money and the resources." He wasn't attempting to intimidate her, simply wanted her to know what she was up against. That's what he did in his business life. Let people know that he was a formidable adversary. At the same time, he didn't want her to hate him. That was the crux of it. They were going to have to work together in this situation—agree on what was best for their niece.

He cleared his throat, cleared his mind. "My grandfather is old, in his seventies now. My parents died when Kent and I were young. It was just the three of us for years, until Kent died, then it became just the two of us. I wasn't aware of Katie Jo until two weeks ago."

She sucked in a breath of air, but made no sign of responding verbally.

"I'm not proud to say it, but my grandfather forced Kent to marry Alice." He chose not to explain that the marriage had been a business deal. Alice's father was a senator and promised the marriage would greatly benefit the East Central Railroad's ability to remain the largest railroad in the nation.

"Kent and Alice left for Europe the day after their wedding. Six weeks later, they were in Ireland when the fire happened." Once again, he chose not to explain the trip to Europe was for Kent to attend a worldwide rail exposition. Everything his family did was always for the railroad.

"I am sorry for your loss," she said quietly.

"Thank you. Two weeks ago, at the Thanksgiving table, my grandfather told me that Kent had told him about Sherri, about her being pregnant. He asked me to find her and the child, bring them to Baltimore for Christmas."

Once again, her eyes widened. She shook her head.

"I fully understand numerous reasons why you wouldn't want to do that, but I'd also like to offer you reasons why you should."

"You can save your breath. There are none," she said.

"There is one very main one," he replied. "Katie Jo is a Cavanaugh. The only Cavanaugh of the next generation. There are benefits and resources that go along with that."

"I provide for her."

"I'm not saying you don't, but do you think you have the right to deny Katie Jo her heritage? Deny her the life she is entitled to live?"

pink "—Elanor wanted to know why I wasn't nursing Katie Jo. I was afraid if I told her the truth, that somehow our location would get back to your brother, so I said she was my sister. That my mother died giving birth to her and that my father had died a few months before then, and that we'd lost our housing because of that."

A knot twisted in his stomach. The Pinkerton agent had told him other things that he hadn't known. Including how her father had worked for the East Central Railroad, in the yards where she'd worked in the restaurant, and that he'd died when she and her sister were young. Her mother had died before then, and when Harper quit her job, without someone working for the company, she had lost her housing. He would make sure that she never had to worry about that again. Ever.

Her explanation made perfect sense. "I'm sorry for all you've been through. I'm sure no one knows what they would have done in your situation, other than act on instinct." He let that settle before continuing, "However, concerning our current situation, I must be perfectly clear. It is not my *wish* to see that my grandfather and Katie Jo spend Christmas together. It is what is going to happen."

He couldn't allow himself to be affected by the way her eyes narrowed or the way her breasts behind the blue-and-white-striped dress rose and fell more quickly. "I'm hoping we can come to an agreement on the best way for that to happen, but if we, you and I, can't come to an agreement, Katie Jo, alone, will be leaving with me on the four o'clock stage tomorrow afternoon."

Disgust filled her face. "That had to be the shortest-lived promise ever made."

He knew full well what she was referencing. "I'm not taking her away from you. I'll bring her back after Christmas. She can live with you for as long as she wants, but be assured, now that I know about her, I will be in her life. She is a Cavanaugh."

She pinched her lips together while shooting him another glare. "Her last name is Hollister."

"Whatever last name she currently uses does not concern me." He leaned forward in his chair, just to demonstrate how serious he was about the situation. "She is my niece as much as she is yours. My responsibility as much as yours, and I will see to that responsibility for the rest of my life. She will receive every benefit of being a member of my family."

Harper was shaking all over again. This time from anger. He would ruin their lives, hers and Katie Jo's. She knew from Sherri's mistake what the Cavanaughs were like, and that was a mistake that she would not repeat. A person couldn't trust anything they said, any promises they made. Kurt had just proven that. Out of one side of his mouth he'd said that he would never take Katie Jo away from her, and out of the other, he'd said that he was taking her to Baltimore for Christmas.

Christmas! Katie Jo was so excited for the holiday that she could barely sit still. Right now, she was making the sugar cookies that she'd been talking about since Thanksgiving. She'd already made a bird feeder for Mrs. Crumb, and had been saving the nearly empty rolls of string from the store to hang the ornaments she planned on making for the tree that Mr. Johnson would cut down for them, as he did each year.

It would break her heart to miss all of that. To miss the school pageant... Feeling the tiniest bit of hope, Harper leaned forward, much like he had. "Part of being responsible for Katie Jo includes her schooling. Even you must understand how missing two weeks of school would hinder her education, her studies."

"Even me?"

"Yes. Even you. So perhaps next summer, she could—"

"She's leaving with me tomorrow, Harper. I'll hire a tutor for the time she's in Baltimore to make sure she doesn't fall behind."

Her teeth stung from how hard she clamped them together. He thinks he has an answer for everything, that he can have his way no matter what. She had to think of something. There had to be a way to prevent this from happening. It would be impossible to stop it completely, but… "If your grandfather is so set upon meeting her, he can come here, for Christmas Day."

"No, she will be going to Baltimore with me, to-morrow," he repeated. "You are welcome to join us, to be with her the entire time." He lifted a single brow. "And to be the one to tell her the truth about her parents."

Every part of her went cold. Chilled clear to the bone. "You can't expect a six-year-old to under-stand—"

"I expect my niece to know the truth. To know she will be meeting her great-grandfather. Spending Christmas with him at his house."

Harper felt as if the entire world was crashing down on her.

"She also needs to know that she has a choice," he said.

The pressure on her, the chill in her bones, in-creased. "Choice about what?"

"If she would like to live in Baltimore, at my house, year-round."

Harper's stomach felt as if it hit the floor, and so

did her hope that she might have a chance at winning. It wasn't even a battle. He outmatched her one thousand to one. He also proved that a man's looks meant nothing. A handsome one could be just as mean and nasty as a homely one.

"You would be welcome to live with her, for as long as you wanted. The house is large. You'd have your own suite of rooms."

It wasn't a suite of rooms she wanted. It was her niece.

If only she'd been better prepared for this.

If only…

Who was she trying to fool? There were no if-onlys.

She'd told herself that she'd never again live off the pittance of a salary from a business that didn't care about anything except its profits. Never depend on anyone but herself. He may have won this battle, but the war wasn't over. She would find a way to fight, to win. Had to. It might not be easy, but Katie Jo was worth whatever scars were caused.

Meeting his gaze, she stated, "We will go with you to Baltimore for Christmas, but there will be a few rules."

He gave a slight nod of acknowledgment.

She held up one finger. "One, I will be the one to tell Katie Jo the truth." She added another finger.

"Two, we will return here after Christmas." She held up a third finger. "Three, when it comes to all aspects of her care, I have the final say."

After a silent moment of waiting, he asked, "Are there more? Four or five? An entire handful?"

Her disgust for him increased, partially because she was working hard to propose more rules. She was certain things would come up, therefore she said, "I'll let you know when they arise." She couldn't think of a reason to remain in his presence, so she stood. "Good night, Mr. Cavanaugh."

He was at her side before she was halfway across the room. Granted, it was a small room. Made even smaller by his presence.

"I'll escort you home," he said.

It felt as if the earth had opened up and she was falling into a big, dark cavern. She had to find something to grasp hold of, pull herself up and get on solid ground again. That wouldn't happen with him nearby. "Why? You obviously know everything there is to know about me and Katie Jo. Therefore, you know that we live above the store, which is next door."

"I do, and will still escort you."

They arrived at the office door at the same time, but he grasped the knob before she could. Miffed, she turned and faced him. "No, you won't. You may be Katie Jo's uncle, but you are nothing to me, nor will

you ever be. You will not control me. No man will *ever control me.*" Watching what her sister had gone through, unable to find anything that had made a dif- ference to Sherri, anything that had helped, Harper had determined that no man would ever do that to her. "I watched a Cavanaugh not only ruin my sis- ter's life but take it from her, and I will not let that happen to Katie Jo."

Even though his hand was on the knob, she grabbed it, pulled the door open and marched out.

Harper didn't stop at the front door, either. Just opened it and walk out into the night. It was now completely dark, and her already chilled body felt colder when surrounded by the icy air.

Kurt was watching her; she knew that without looking back, so she kept her hands at her sides, rather than using them to rub some warmth into her arms, and kept walking to the edge of the building. There, she turned and, once out of his sight, ran the length of the walkway between the two buildings. Then she raced up the stairway to her apartment and shot inside. The familiar darkness provided no relief. Though some heat penetrated in...

from the stove...

Normally, she went upstairs each afternoon and started a fire in the coal stove half an hour before closing time, so the apartment was warm for Katie Jo when she entered it. She hadn't done that today.

She did so now, first lighting an oil lamp, then building a fire in the coal stove. It would take time before the heat began to chase aside the chill, so she sat down at the table and indulged in something she hadn't done for a very long time.

Burying her face in her hands, she cried.

She had never rushed to wait on Kurt back at the restaurant, but her heart had pounded every time he'd walked through the door, and a warm flush had [...] over her entire body when he'd wait until a [...]ble in her area. It wasn't as if they'd [...] just warned him about what [...]ght when

four rooms that consisted of two bedrooms, a bathing room and the larger space that was both the kitchen and sitting area.

[...]tore below, it wasn't enough to warm the [...]up into the apartment

adding a chunk of coal to the stove, she hurried across the alley to the Johnson's house.

Katie Jo was elbow deep in a huge bowl of dough, and though Harper felt an urgency to get her home, she also didn't know how she would tell Katie Jo that she'd been lying to her for her entire young life.

They would be leaving tomorrow, there was no stopping that, and Harper chose to let Katie Jo enjoy the cookie making to the fullest.

She and Katie Jo also ate supper with Elanor and Wayne, and it was obvious that Elanor knew something wasn't right. Harper would have to tell them that she and Katie Jo would be leaving tomorrow. They depended upon her at the store, and she hated the idea of letting them down.

When the meal was finished and the kitchen put back in order, Harper sent Katie Jo to get her coat. "I need to speak with you, but it needs to wait until morning," she told Elanor.

Elanor gave her a heartfelt hug. "You have friends here, many friends, who will help you, whatever it is you need."

Harper returned Elanor's hug, but knew that all the friends in the world couldn't stop Kurt. She highly doubted that he'd ever failed at anything.

Chapter Four

Life in the mind of a child held a simple, self-centered logic. As it should be, and Harper was thankful that Katie Jo wasn't overly upset by anything she'd been told. Truthfully, she was elated at the idea of going to Baltimore.

That wasn't surprising. Katie Jo had wanted to ride on a train for years. When her fascination with trains had first appeared, Harper had wondered if Katie Jo had somehow inherited it from Kent, because the only time she'd been on one had been when she was a tiny infant.

Harper hadn't attempted to quell her niece's fixation and had assured her that someday she would travel on a train.

This morning, it was clear that Katie Jo understood what it would mean not to be in Pine City for Christmas. As soon as she finished her breakfast, she wrapped the bird feeder she'd made for Mrs. Crumb by rolling a pine cone in molasses, bread crumbs and dry oatmeal.

Elanor wasn't upset over the news and was so encouraging about the entire ordeal that Harper felt more alone than ever. Not that she'd expected Elanor to be able to stop it from happening, but her positivity was so contrary to the dread plaguing Harper. She was afraid, so afraid of what could happen there.

To both herself and Katie Jo.

As it had been all night, Kurt's mind was still on Harper's final words yesterday evening, about how a Cavanaugh had not only ruined, but had taken her sister's life. He couldn't fight the truth of that. Halfway through the dark night, he'd questioned leaving Pine City alone, telling his grandfather that they had no right to interfere in Katie Jo's life now.

He'd chosen not to do that, because in the end, Katie Jo was a Cavanaugh and deserved the benefits that could come from that. Wealth, if nothing else. Enough that Harper could own a house and worry about nothing more than taking care of Katie Jo. But money wasn't the answer to everything. He'd known that his entire life.

Waiting near the corner of the hotel, he stepped forward as Harper and Katie Jo walked out of the store's front door. "Good morning."

"Good morning!" Katie Jo instantly replied.

Once again, she was bundled in her red coat, hat and mittens, and the smile on her cherub face had him glancing at Harper, wondering if she had told Katie Jo the truth.

Harper's slight nod was barely noticeable. Possibly because Katie Jo was explaining the package in her hands, wrapped in brown paper and tied with a red ribbon.

"I have to give this to Mrs. Crumb on my way to school," she said. "It's a bird feeder for her to hang on her porch and watch the birds out of her window. She likes birds."

"It sounds like she does, and I'm sure she'll like your present," he said. "Would you mind if I walked to school with you?"

"You can do that, if you want." She glanced up at Harper and waited for a nod, before looking at him again as they began walking. "Did you know that you're my uncle?"

"I did know that," he answered.

"I've never had an uncle before," she said. "Sophie Watters has an uncle. He has hair growing out of his nose." Using a mittened finger, she stuck it in a tiny nostril to show him.

Harper cleared her throat, which caused Katie Jo

to look up and quickly drop her finger upon seeing Harper shake her head.

Kurt had to pinch his lips together when Katie Jo looked up at him again and nodded, as if to confirm that the man really did have hair growing out of his nose, but also that she couldn't talk about it any longer. He gave her a wink and felt his heart flutter at how her smile grew. Then, he brought the conversation back to her statement. "I'm happy that I'm your uncle. I've never had a niece before."

She grinned, then with a slight frown, asked, "Do you have any of your own kids?"

"No, I do not."

"Why?"

"Because I'm not married."

She nodded, as if that explained it all, and asked, "Should I call you Uncle?"

"I don't see why not," he replied.

She looked up at Harper again and, upon receiving a nod, nodded herself. "I think I'll call you Uncle Kurt. Sophie calls her uncle, Uncle Todd."

"I like the sound of that. And what would you like me to call you?"

Her mouth twisted, as if she was thinking before she explained, "Katie Jo, because Sophie's uncle just calls her Sophie, not Niece Sophie."

"Very well, then, Katie Jo it is."

"Did you know that I have a great-grandpa, too? And that I'm going to ride on a train to see him? I've never been on a train before, but it was one of the hopes in my hope chest. Harper is going to tell Miss Carpenter that I won't be at school for two weeks, because we'll be in Baltimore. I've never been there before. Have you?"

"Yes, I have."

"Do they have a school there?"

"They do."

"Maybe I could go to school there. I'm an exceptional speller. That's what Miss Carpenter says. Exceptional for my age. I like spelling tests. We won't have one of those today. We had it yesterday. Today we'll—"

She continued to tell him about what would happen in school today, and about some of the other children, as they walked. He thoroughly enjoyed listening to her every word, all the while wondering how Harper was faring. She looked fine.

Actually, she looked extraordinarily lovely. Her coat was brown, a light brown, with a darker brown fur collar that nearly matched the color of her eyes. The conversation she'd had with Katie Jo had to have been difficult. He would have gladly joined her, assisted in explaining things, but understood her preference to do it alone. He respected her for that. Respected her for all she'd done for Katie Jo.

He held regret for not checking into why she stopped working at the restaurant years ago. Had he done that, he would have known that she quit because her sister was ill and needed to be taken care of and that she'd moved away after Sherri had given birth.

He couldn't find fault in how she blamed Kent, nor was there anything he could do about it. The best he could hope for was that she'd come to understand that he wouldn't fail her or Katie Jo.

Katie Jo talked until she ran up the walkway to a house where an older woman stood on the front porch. After handing over the package, Katie Jo pointed at him, and he couldn't deny his chest puffed up at the smile on his niece's face. The woman had questions in her eyes but withheld asking them. As did the teacher at the school.

During their walk back to the store, he considered questioning Harper on what she'd said for Katie Jo to be so accepting of him and the trip, but chose instead for her to have the time she needed to process everything.

At the store, he purchased their stage tickets and gave Mr. Johnson extra funds, with the instructions that it was to pay for whatever Harper or Katie Jo may need for their stay in Baltimore.

With a nod at Harper, he walked to the door. Whether she knew it or not, there was a look of thanks in her eyes, and he took the rush of warmth that flooded his body as a warning. He needed to be cautious. When they first met, all those years ago, his grandfather had been pressuring him and Kent to get married. He'd had no interest, until he saw her. She was the only woman to ever spark something inside of him.

Then there had been Kent's sudden wedding to Alice, their untimely deaths, and when Harper had no longer been working at the depot restaurant, he told himself that it was for the best. For the best if she had married someone else.

The only thing Kent had said upon his wedding was that he was doing it for the East Central Railroad, because that's what was expected of a Cavanaugh. That their lives were dedicated to the company and nothing more.

That was the truth, and precisely why Kurt avoided women, relationships of any kind. There was no time in his life for what people called love. Love was a Cavanaugh's curse. It equaled nothing but loss. His parents, his brother, and it had already struck the next generation. Katie Jo had never even known her parents.

Kurt left the store and spent the day receiving scrutinizing looks, while doing little more than exploring the town as a way to use up time. People weren't rude, just curious, because word had spread quickly that Harper and Katie Jo were going to Baltimore with him for Christmas.

When the stage rolled into town, Katie Jo made the old driver laugh aloud with her excitement over riding in his coach. Half of the town laughed, too, because they were either peeking out of windows or standing nearby to say goodbye.

It would just be the three of them traveling, and Katie Jo was the first to climb into the stage. As Kurt held out a hand to assist Harper, he took note of her quick intake of breath and the direction of her gaze. She was looking about as if waiting for someone to save her.

"Shall we?" Kurt asked.

She sighed, nodded and accepted his hand to steady herself as she stepped inside the stage.

Kurt climbed in behind her, took a seat across from the two of them and held his tongue. He didn't trust himself to speak. He'd known his arrival, what had to happen, would disrupt their lives. He'd also known that Harper wasn't married, and now wondered if she'd been waiting for someone specific to emerge from the crowd and challenge him.

If there was such a person, and their roles were

reversed, if some man had arrived to take Harper and Katie Jo away from him, even for two weeks, he would have protested. More than protested. He wouldn't have let it happen.

There were things happening inside him right now that no woman had ever made him feel. He had no right, no reason, to be jealous of another man when it came to Harper, but that's what was there.

That wasn't the only thing, either. He wanted to know what her lips would feel like beneath his. What her body would feel like pressed up against his, or beneath his, her warm breath on his bare skin as they lay together, whispering in the dark.

He'd wondered those same things about her years ago, and it was frustrating to think he was reverting to a younger version of himself, when he hadn't yet known what his future could and couldn't hold. When he hadn't yet understood the family curse.

Glancing out of the window as the stage rolled past the homes and buildings of Pine City, he willed his years of emotional self-discipline to kick back in, to give him the self-control he would need to accomplish this task.

That's what it was. Simply a task that he was required to fulfill. Katie Jo was now the future of the East Central Railroad, the next generation. He had to wonder whether that was the real reason his grandfather wanted her found.

After Kent's marriage, his grandfather had paraded daughters from blue blood families before him with renewed focus, desperately seeking an appropriate match. He'd told his grandfather that his efforts were fruitless. That he would not marry, have children, just to solidify the future of the railroad. He would turn the company over to the employees, who were the backbone, the real reason the company was so successful.

Something Katie Jo said caught his attention. She'd been chattering since they'd climbed into the stage. "Excuse me," he said, interrupting her midsentence. "Did you say someone pulled your hair?"

"Yes," she replied, with her missing teeth slur and her braids bouncing as she nodded. "Wade McMann. He said I thought I was smart because I was going to ride on a train. He said trains are stupid. I told him that trains are not stupid, and that I don't think I'm smart, I know I'm smart, and that if he was smart, he'd let go of my hair." She sucked air to continue. "Because if he didn't let go of my hair, I'd tell the teacher and he'd end up sitting in the corner for the rest of the day."

Although there was satisfaction on her face, Katie Jo glanced at Harper.

With a faint smile, Harper nodded slightly.

Kurt read between the lines. Obviously, Katie Jo had needed to learn how to respond to this boy, or perhaps another child in the past, had learned to use words rather than physically reacting to hair pulling. She had spunk, and he could imagine her giving punch for punch in a schoolyard fight. He could also imagine Harper not approving of that behavior.

If he needed further proof that Katie was his niece, he had it. She may not have been bragging she was a Cavanaugh, but the inherited traits were there. Both he and Kent had been involved in more than one schoolyard argument.

"Does this Wade pick on you often?" he asked.

"He picks on everyone, but I have to be nice to him because—" She stopped as Harper lightly touched her knee. After a deep breath, Katie Jo continued, "Because I need to be nice to everyone."

She clearly wasn't sold on that reasoning, but again, due to something that had taken place in the past, had accepted it. His gaze caught and locked with Harper's, and an understanding flowed between them. Compassion, empathy for this young Wade person. Something in her silent communication told him that the poor boy didn't have a good homelife.

He wasn't sure exactly how he knew that, and Kurt wanted to believe he would have had that same understanding with anyone, but that wasn't true. He felt a connection with Harper. Unlike anything he'd ever known. There was no explanation for that.

Harper couldn't describe the draw she felt toward Kurt, but it scared her. She quickly looked away, out of the window. Pine City had disappeared, and that, too, worried her. She hadn't traveled more than a few miles from town in over six years, and it felt as if she was leaving a part of herself behind.

It was strange, but she'd had to take a final look, to see what she was leaving behind.

Kurt had looked at her as if he knew she was looking for something, almost as if he could read her mind. Like a moment ago when his single nod had told her that he'd understood that Wade McMann couldn't help the way he behaved at times. She hadn't had to voice that Wade's father drank heavily and that Wade was mistreated at times.

Kurt hadn't drawn Wade back into the conversation with Katie Jo, either. Instead, he'd let her comment go and changed the subject, back to trains, which had Katie Jo completely captivated.

Harper found it difficult not to be captivated herself. His knowledge was interesting, and his patience in answering Katie Jo's questions was admirable. A plethora of subjects were discussed, because that's how Katie Jo's mind worked, bouncing about like a rubber ball, and he didn't seem to mind a single question. Nor did he skip over answering any, including whether his grandfather had hair growing out of his nose. Katie Jo noticed little things like that and was vexed over them more than most.

Kurt assured Katie Jo that he'd never noticed hair growing out of his grandfather's nose and, once again, Harper felt a unique connection to him when their gazes caught. She had to smile at the humor in his eyes.

Katie Jo's questions didn't stop once they'd departed the stage and boarded an elegant private train car. Sherri had told Harper about the private car where she'd had dinner with Kent numerous times but, though similar, this one was different. Besides a sitting area and dining area, there was a separate bedroom, with a bathing room and a small kitchen. Glossy wood covered all of the walls, the furnishings were upholstered with thick materials of dark reds, blues and golds, and the plush rugs on the floor were dark green.

"I knew riding on a train was going to be grand," Katie Jo exclaimed, moving from area to area and inspecting every detail. "Grand. Just grand."

"She certainly is an inquisitive child," Kurt said.

His smile was so genuine, Harper's heart nearly did a flip.

"It's wonderful that you haven't stifled that in her," he whispered.

He was so close to her, the warmth of his breath on her neck sent tingles all over her body. She stepped forward, in the direction where Katie Jo had disappeared. "It wasn't for lack of trying." Hurrying, she walked past the tiny kitchen and into the bedroom.

There she found Katie Jo, still wearing her red coat and hat, lying on the bed with her hands behind her head.

"I think I need a little rest," Katie Jo said. "It's all the excitement."

"I think you need to remove your coat, shoes and hat and ask permission before making yourself so comfortable." Harper grasped an arm. "Up you go."

"All right." Katie Jo sighed as she scooted to the edge of the bed. "This sure is grand. The grandest place I've ever seen."

"That is not an excuse to forgo manners."

With a hop off the bed and a skip to the doorway where Kurt stood, Katie Jo asked, "Would it be all right if I took a little rest on your bed?"

Harper pressed a hand to her temple at how Katie Jo exaggerated a yawn.

Kurt grinned as he knelt down in front of Katie Jo.

"Of course, however dinner will arrive momentarily, so I believe you should eat first, then take your rest."

"You mean we are going to eat here?" Katie Jo asked. "In this train car?"

"Yes, we have just enough time to eat before the train departs for Baltimore." Kurt touched the tip of her nose. "It's easier to eat when the train isn't moving."

Harper felt her throat tighten. She'd known that this trip would expose Katie Jo to things that she'd never be able to compete with, and this was just the beginning.

Chapter Five

The meal of tender roast beef, asparagus spears, mashed potatoes with gravy and candied carrots was carried in by several restaurant staff on trays covered with domed silver lids. There were also rolls to mop up the gravy and slices of frosted chocolate cake for dessert. If Harper hadn't known better, she'd have thought that Katie Jo had requested the menu, minus the asparagus, which, as were the rules, Katie Jo tasted and determined that maybe she'd grow to like it someday, but not this day.

After the dishes were removed by more staff, Harper assisted Katie Jo to settle onto the bed and was left with no real excuse to remain in the bedroom. Her nerves were so heightened, she felt as if she was about to take flight. It was a chore to simply put one foot in front of the other, and she couldn't blame it on the movement of the train.

The miniature parlor stove had already been lit

when they'd arrived, which had been a welcome relief after the cold stage ride. The entire car was now toasty warm, and that meant Kurt had removed his overcoat and suit jacket and rolled up the sleeves of his white shirt.

Harper tried to divert her gaze as she walked into the sitting area, but her eyes roamed right back to him. He was sitting in a dark red, high-back armchair, reading a newspaper, which he quickly folded and set aside.

He stood and gestured toward an identical chair, separated from his by a small table. A row of windows was behind the chairs, and even though the curtains were open, nothing could be seen outside because darkness had fallen before they'd arrived at the train station.

"Would you care for something to drink?" he asked.

"No, thank you," she replied while sitting. "I'm fine."

He sat in his chair. "I doubt that you're fine, Harper."

The way he said her name was no different than when anyone else said it, yet it affected her far differently. And, no, she wasn't fine. She would never be fine again. He was the reason. Seeing him made her remember old foolish dreams. Dreams that she had put behind her. That irritated her as much as everything else. "What would you prefer that I say?" She kept her voice low, due to Katie Jo's close proximity. "That I'd rather be back in Pine City? That I wish you'd never found us? Because then I would be fine."

"I understand that. I understand how I've disrupted your life, but you had to believe that at some point your secret would be discovered."

She had known that. It was something she'd thought about a great deal, yet she shook her head at his disbelief. "Have you thought this through? I mean really thought it through, what people are going to say when all of a sudden you have a niece? You're unmarried and only had one brother, only one way to become an uncle. How are you going to explain that?" Shaking her head again, she added, "Did you think about how that will affect Katie Jo? Having all of the Baltimore blue bloods talking about her behind her back?"

"I'll protect her."

"Protect her?" Harper sucked in a breath. She'd heard enough stories about Baltimore's affluent upper class. More than enough to know that she didn't want anything to do with any of them. They were a society all of their own.

"Yes, I will protect her, and you."

"I don't need your protection, and Katie Jo shouldn't, either."

"Katie Jo shouldn't be denied what is rightfully

hers." He was keeping his voice hushed, too, and leaned closer. "Neither you nor I have the right to do that to her."

"Nor do we have the right to put her in dangerous situations," she replied.

"She won't be in any danger."

"How can you say that? People can be ruthless. She's only six years old."

"Because anyone who would be disparaging about her would be insulting the entire Cavanaugh family, and that is something they would regret."

She shook her head at his ignorance. "That may be a fine thought while sitting in your ivory tower, but it's not reality." Still whispering, she continued, "Reality is that the rich get richer off the backs of the poor, and when the blue bloods learn that you have an illegitimate niece whose mother was a waitress, nothing will stop them from making disparaging remarks. Not you or anyone else. She'll be branded for life."

"I give you my solemn promise—"

"Promise? How many of those do you give in one breath and break in the next?"

He leaned back in his chair, looked at her. It wasn't a mean or angry look. Just simply a look, almost like he wasn't sure what to say. She didn't know if that was the case or not. His calm, even disposition was hard to read. There were times when she instinctively knew what he was thinking, and then, times like this, when she didn't have a clue.

"What would you suggest we do in this situation?" he asked.

That was simple. "I would suggest that you let us travel back to Pine City, tell your grandfather you couldn't find Katie Jo and forget all about us."

"That's not an option," he said. "Try again."

"It is," she argued. "You just refuse to see it."

"And you refuse to see things my way."

"Because I don't want to see my niece get hurt."

"Neither do I," he said. "Which gives us one very important thing in common."

Frustration, along with a deep sense of disappointment, washed over her. "You and I will never have anything in common."

"I disagree, Harper. I believe the two of us have a lot in common."

What she saw in his eyes momentarily stunned her. There was not only honesty; there was something deeper. Hope? Yearning? She wasn't sure what, but it touched her heart. Made it flutter. Her mind, however, had to remain realistic. "We're from two different worlds."

"There is only one world, but there are different perspectives. What you said earlier about the rich getting richer off the backs of the poor is one of them.

Not everyone sees it that way, but I do. Which is why, since taking over all aspects of East Central, I've implemented policies and regulations to ensure safer work environments, better wages and a cap on required work hours."

A shiver of disbelief washed over her. No one would believe changes like that had come from an owner, especially a Cavanaugh, and there was no way for him to know she'd imagined changes just like that. "You have?"

"I have, and I intend to do more, but implementing every change is an uphill battle. There is opposition coming from all directions." He gave her a slight nod. "That only makes me more dedicated to make the changes. It's for the future, not just of the railroad, but of America. Men, and women, have fought for this country several times in the past, and it's our job, all of us, to build upon our freedom for all to prosper."

Despite all she knew, all she believed, it was impossible to put a damper on her eagerness to know more. For years, she'd thought about how different her life could have been if her family's livelihood hadn't been so tied to the railroad.

"Will you answer a question for me?" he asked.

She nodded.

"What exactly are you so afraid of happening to Katie Jo?"

Harper opened her mouth, ready to spew a plethora of things she worried about for Katie Jo, but didn't, because those were everyday concerns she'd had for years. Things like Katie Jo catching pneumonia, or falling and getting hurt. He wasn't asking about those things. He was asking specifically about him and his family. That worry had also been there for years, but even the thought of saying it made her feel vulnerable. It would be an admission of her inabilities. She looked away, considered not answering, but maybe if he knew, he'd understand and let them return to Pine City.

"I'm afraid of her getting her hopes up, of Katie Jo believing that someone could change her life, make all of her dreams come true, and then being abandoned. Leaving her with a heart so broken it can't be repaired." She hadn't been able to stop it from happening to Sherri, and was terrified that she wouldn't be able to stop it from happening to Katie Jo, either.

Kurt wasn't surprised by her answer. However, he was stunned by the strength of the pain that struck his heart. Sherri hadn't been the only one hurt. Harper had been, too. She'd lost all she'd had, her life destroyed, yet she'd found the ability, the will, to go on and make a new life for her and Katie Jo. The last thing he wanted was for her to believe that he would let that happen to her again, or to Katie Jo. Although, he could understand why she feared that was exactly what was happening.

He reached across the small table between them, laid a hand on her shoulder. "That is something else we have in common, Harper. I don't want a repeat of what happened to your sister. That was unfair and cruel. Cruel to your sister, to you, to Katie Jo, and whether you believe it or not, it was cruel to me. I was denied a niece, family, for almost seven years. I would have helped you from the very beginning had I known. That's my goal now, to help you and Katie Jo, and I believe we can accomplish that, together."

She had closed her eyes, as if she couldn't look at him. Why? Because she thought he was lying? She had reason to believe that after what she'd been through. And despite meeting years ago, their interactions had been limited, leaving them not truly knowing each other.

"You gave me three rules yesterday," he said quietly, "including that you have final say in all aspects of Katie's care. I will follow those rules, but I am asking for one thing in return."

She opened her eyes, which shimmered with unshed tears. "What is that?"

"That you believe me. Believe I'm being honest with you. That everything I'm doing is in Katie Jo's best interest." He rubbed her shoulder. "I believe in you. I believe you are afraid, and I thank you for voicing your fears. In order to ease some of your concerns, we don't need to tell anyone that Katie Jo is my niece. We will know, my grandfather and household staff will know, but other than that, we can say she is your sister. We'll simply let people believe the two of you are friends of the family who are joining us for Christmas."

She gasped slightly as her eyes widened, then she shook her head and whispered, "Katie Jo knows, and she..." She shook her head again.

"I'll talk to her about that." He gave her shoulder a slight squeeze. "Actually, *we'll* talk to her about it. I believe that we need to agree to put our own preconceptions aside and work together in her best interest."

A tiny frown knit her brows together as she blinked several times, contemplating his request. Just as she opened her mouth to respond, the train whistle blew.

Her smile was quick, spontaneous, and he grinned in return, because he'd heard the same thing that she had. At the first sound of the whistle, there'd been a thump and then the quick pitter-patter of running feet.

"Are we there?" Katie Jo asked, running into the room on stocking-covered feet. "In Baltimore?"

Kurt caught her with both hands when she couldn't stop and slid toward his chair. He plopped her onto his lap. "No, we aren't there yet. The train will make several stops before we arrive in Baltimore. It'll be well after midnight by then." He touched the tip of her button nose. "How was your rest?"

She let out a long sigh while smiling. "I pretended like I was lying on a cloud, floating through the sky. Have you ever done that?"

He didn't have a lot of experience with children, but this one was a pure delight. "No, I can't say that I have."

"You should try it. You, too, Harper. It made my heart happy."

The way Harper's face softened when she looked at Katie Jo affected his entire being. He knew he'd never seen a more beautiful woman. There was something mystical about the way her eyes sparkled. It was clear that, though Katie Jo had lost her mother, no one would ever love her more than Harper.

"I will have to try that," Harper said.

Kurt pulled his gaze off her and asked Katie Jo, "Does that mean you are enjoying your train ride?"

"I am, very much, but there's one thing that I'm wondering about," she answered.

"What's that?" he asked.

"Why didn't we get a ticket to ride the train?"

"Well, remember I told you that we'd be riding in a private car, not in the passenger car?" When she nodded, he continued, "The train is paid to pull the entire car, no matter how many people are in it, so that's why you didn't get a ticket."

She let out a long sigh. "I sure was hoping for a ticket to put in my hope chest."

"I will get you a ticket for your chest," he said.

"You will? How?"

He chuckled at her inquisitiveness. "I will request one from the porter. Now, tell me, what else is in this hope chest of yours?"

"Well, let's see, there's a matchstick from when I hoped I'd be old enough to light a lamp, and a doll shoe from when I hoped for a doll for my birthday last year. I lost one of her shoes and she looked silly only wearing one shoe. And there's a…"

He glanced at Harper as Katie Jo chattered on about all of her treasures, and the smile on Harper's face said she didn't feel sorry for him. He'd asked, and when Katie Jo was asked a question, she answered it in its entirety.

With a nod to Harper, he turned back to Katie Jo, and listened about feathers and a rock, hair ribbons and several other items, before being told that she would show him the hope chest, but couldn't right now because it was in their luggage. She then revealed that Harper also had a hope chest.

"She does?" he asked, glancing at Harper, who had

let out a small sigh. Many women had hope chests that they filled with items for when they got married, and he couldn't help but wonder if Harper was hoping for marriage. Most women did.

"Yes. It's big. Mine's little. Mr. Johnson made it for me, but Harper has had hers for a long time. It's at the foot of her bed and she sits on it to put on her shoes."

"Does she?" When Katie Jo bobbed her head, he asked, "And what is in Harper's hope chest?"

"Nothing." Katie Jo sighed. "It's where she puts our winter coats during the summer, and clothes that are too small for me until we can find someone to give them to." With a shrug, she added, "Harper doesn't have any hopes."

"Everyone has hopes," he said, still wondering if there were other things in Harper's hope chest. "I know Harper has many hopes about you."

Katie Jo looked at Harper. "You do?"

"I do. I hope you do well in school. I hope you are kind to people. I hope you will eat your vegetables, and—"

"Those aren't hopes," Katie Jo said, huffing out a long breath. "They're rules."

Kurt laughed and planted a quick kiss on Katie Jo's hair. "That's because she hopes you'll follow the rules."

The train had come to a stop and the knock that

sounded on the door would be his man, Abner. Kurt had introduced Harper and Katie Jo to him upon arrival at the train station. "Come in."

"Excuse me, sir." Abner removed his flat-topped hat and nodded toward Harper. "Miss Hollister." With another nod toward Katie Jo, he said, "Miss Katie Jo. We will be at the station for approximately twenty minutes. Is there anything I can get for you?"

Kurt looked at Harper first. She shook her head. Katie Jo grimaced and shrugged one little shoulder.

"What is it you would like?" Kurt asked her.

"I've never seen a train station," she said. "We got in this car before I'd even gotten a peek."

"Then go get your coat and shoes," Kurt said.

Chapter Six

Kurt couldn't remember if he'd ever walked through a train station for pleasure, but he was now, and it was indeed pleasurable. Katie Jo was amusing him just being her inquisitive self, but she was also making Harper laugh, and that truly was unforgettable. Her face was alight and her soft laughter hung in the air like musical notes. It was obvious that what made Harper happy was seeing Katie Jo happy.

He wanted to know what else brought Harper joy. She was so beautiful, he couldn't stop from staring and had to ball his hands into fists to keep from touching her. The uncanny attraction he felt for her was being amplified minute by minute. Pulling his attention away from her was nearly impossible, even though that was what he needed to do. This wasn't about him or Harper, it was about Katie Jo and what she deserved.

The station wasn't overly large, nor was there much

to see, yet Katie Jo was making the most of it. "Does she ever slow down?" he asked Harper.

"Yes, she's always slept well."

He chuckled. "Because she wears herself out during the day."

"She does." Harper's eyes were on her niece, who was listening intently to the station manager explaining the train routes and schedules. "You know we can't expect her to go back to saying she and I are sisters."

"I do." He'd figured that out by the fifth time Katie Jo had called him Uncle Kurt since entering the station. This was turning out to be more difficult than he'd imagined, and he knew why. Harper was affecting him far more than he'd expected. He'd known that he'd see her as soon as he got the report from the Pinkerton agent, but hadn't considered it an issue due to his ability to hide his emotions, even from himself. He was failing at that because he hadn't taken Harper into account. Not just her beauty, but all of her. Her life, her hopes.

He didn't want to ruin her life. He wanted to make it better. To help. But her hope chest was probably full of things for when she got married, and she'd want to have Katie Jo live with her.

Why did his thoughts keep going back to marriage? That wasn't like him.

However, he knew his grandfather, and seeing Katie Jo once, for two weeks, was not going to be enough. His grandfather had a grander plan, as he always did, and going against him was going to be a battle. It always was.

There was a lot of truth in what Harper had said about Katie Jo being singled out as his niece. He normally didn't put much thought into what people said, but he would this time. The Cavanaugh name, the East Central Railroad, even he, himself, could withstand a scandal or two, but not if it played havoc on Harper's and Katie Jo's lives. He'd figure it all out. How to help, without ruining their lives. And without ruining his own in the process.

Giving the small of Harper's back a gentle pat, he left her side to walk over and scoop Katie Jo up off the floor near the map on the wall. "Time for us to return to the car. We don't want to hold up the train."

There was enough doubt in Harper's brown eyes when he turned around to make him half consider taking them back home. That wouldn't solve anything though, it would merely postpone it. Harper pulled up a smile for her niece when Katie Jo began explaining the number of stops between the station and Baltimore as he carried her toward the door.

That conversation continued as they walked to the train car, but once inside, Katie Jo switched gears and began asking him questions about Baltimore, including his house and who lived there with him.

"Well, there is my grandfather, Axel, and our cook, Samuel Borst, our butler, Lincoln Ford, and our housekeeper, Mrs. Wagner, and a few other maids and kitchen workers." He waited as Harper helped Katie Jo remove her coat, before he added, "And Paws."

"Paws?" Katie Jo's eyes shone even brighter. "Who is Paws?"

"He is a black-and-white dog that showed up at our house about three years ago." Kurt took both Katie Jo's and Harper's coats and hung them on the hooks in the small closet, along with his own. "He was just a pup, and we tried to find his owner but couldn't, so he's lived with us ever since."

"A dog." Katie Jo's sigh echoed throughout the train car.

The way Harper had a fingertip pressed against one temple had him asking, "Let me guess. A dog is in your hope chest?"

Katie Jo giggled. "A dog wouldn't fit in it."

"But it was one of your hopes?" he asked.

She shrugged. "I can't tell you that."

"Why not?"

"Because if I tell people my hopes, they might not come true."

Trying to fully understand her reasoning, he said, "If you don't tell people, no one will be able to help you make your hopes come true."

"No one needs to help me make them come true," she explained. "They come true all on their own. Like when I hoped Joshua would let me shoot his sling-shot—he lives in the house by Mr. and Mrs. Johnson—and sure enough, one day he waved at me and asked me if I wanted to shoot it. I did, and I saved the rock, put it in my chest."

Kurt may never have met someone so faithful to her own beliefs. "Let me get this straight, the hopes in your hope chest are things that have already come true?"

She nodded.

"What about those that haven't?"

"They are in here." She pointed to her chest. "In my heart."

The breath Harper hadn't realized she was holding gushed out when Kurt looked at her. Her normally clear mind was so fog-filled she was having a hard time forming a single thought. Other than thoughts about him. Thoughts that she'd long ago buried so deep she was sure they'd been forgotten.

They hadn't.

The train car jolted as the wheels began to move, and unprepared, Harper was jostled, and nearly lost her footing. She might have, if Kurt hadn't grasped her upper arms to steady her.

Her hands ended up on his chest, and for the life of her, she couldn't pull them away. All she could do was stare up at him and pray that he couldn't read her mind. She used to dream about kissing him, and those dreams had renewed themselves the moment she'd seen him, becoming stronger with each passing minute.

She closed her eyes, wishing it was that easy to block out the images inside her mind. It was maddening. She was no longer a young girl who believed in the impossible. There was a time when she'd been envious of her sister for having captured the love of a Cavanaugh.

Harper pinched her lips together. She now knew that Sherri hadn't captured love, she'd been taken advantage of, and that would not be repeated. Not by her, or by Katie Jo.

Collecting her wits, she pushed away from his chest and took a step back.

"Are you all right?" he asked.

She took another step back, and another, until he had to release her upper arms. "Yes. I just wasn't prepared..." She let her voice fade away and glanced at where Katie Jo had climbed up on one of the armchairs and was sitting on her knees, leaning over the back of the chair and staring out of the window as the train pulled away from the station.

"Uncle Kurt, is Paws a big dog or a little dog?" she asked, never turning from the window.

"I'd say he's a medium-sized dog," Kurt answered.

Harper's heart sank a little deeper. Of course, he'd have a dog. There was no conceivable way to prevent Katie Jo from being hurt when this all ended. And it would end. In two weeks, they would return to their old lives in Pine City, but nothing would be the same.

Ever.

Katie Jo would experience things in the next two weeks that would make her want far more than their simple life. There had been a time when she'd wanted different things, too, until she realized what that would cost.

Harper took a seat on the small sofa across from the chairs where Kurt and Katie Jo sat, talking about the dog and other things that she would discover upon arrival at his home. Though the train chugged along at a rapid speed, time appeared to crawl. She wasn't in a hurry to arrive at his home, but she did want more space than the train car provided. Kurt being so near made it impossible for her to think straight. Thinking of a way to protect both herself and Katie Jo from his charms was her only hope.

Katie Jo was hanging on his every word, and

Harper wasn't much better herself. Despite all she knew, the sound of his voice did things to her insides, and she didn't dare meet his gaze again. Didn't dare look at him for fear of the desires that would surface.

Dear Lord, but this train couldn't get to Baltimore fast enough.

That happened shortly after midnight and, to Harper's surprise, Katie Jo was still awake. It could have been excitement, but Harper knew it was also because she'd never suggested that Katie Jo go to sleep. She would have been left alone with Kurt, and that was something she would avoid during the next two weeks.

Completely avoid.

By the time they'd put on their coats and Kurt opened the train car door, there was already a horse-drawn carriage parked next to the car. Abner and another man, who turned out to be the driver, Tony Allen, loaded the two bags of luggage that Harper had packed for her and Katie Jo into the back of the carriage, while Kurt escorted them onto a seat and gave them thick blankets.

The two seats in the open carriage faced each other, and the lap blankets were large enough for Katie Jo to cocoon herself in one of them. The elegance of the carriage wasn't lost on Katie Jo, who oohed and aahed over every detail, including the matching white horses.

Kurt sat opposite them as they rolled through streets crowded with traffic and hosting well-lit buildings. The further away from the station they traveled, the quieter things became, and once they crossed a bridge, the only thing breaking the silence was the noise of the horses and carriage. The bright moonlight glistened off a layer of newly fallen snow. Harper had never visited the city, nor neighborhoods like this, but the large homes set far back from the road and a fair distance apart from each other told her this was where the blue bloods lived.

When she was a waitress at the depot, the trains had carried many blue blood families from Baltimore to Philadelphia and New York, where they went to show off their wealth, happily belittling those who had to work for a living. The last thing she wanted was for Katie Jo to experience the impertinence she'd witnessed.

"It's not much further," Kurt said.

"I sure hope Paws likes me," Katie Jo said.

"He will," Kurt replied. "Everyone will."

Katie Jo was a joy and everyone did like her, but that was in Pine City. Here, Harper feared it would be different. People wouldn't like her just because of how she'd come to be, which was so unfair. If she'd been born as a Cavanaugh, it would be a completely different story. Then she'd be accepted everywhere she went.

She was a child. A wonderful, adorable little girl who should never be singled out for something that was beyond her control. It frustrated her that Kurt knew all that, yet he was willing to go ahead with this.

The carriage turned a corner, and based on the number of windows lit up on the massive house at the end of the long driveway, everyone in the Cavanaugh household must have waited up for their arrival.

Harper had never considered herself a fearful person, but there were so many things she was afraid of about this situation that her entire being was trembling.

The elaborately carved front door opened as the carriage rolled to a stop. With a shaggy black-and-white dog by his side, an older man, who had to be Axel Cavanaugh, stepped out onto the wide, covered porch. Harper had never met the man, but had heard plenty about the great railroad baron, and none of it led her to believe he was an overly pleasant man.

"Is that Paws?" Katie Joe discarded the lap blanket and shot to her feet.

Kurt flipped down the step and climbed out. "Yes, it is."

Harper folded both blankets and sent up a silent prayer that the next two weeks would pass quickly.

"Will he let me pet him?" Katie Jo asked as Kurt lifted her out of the carriage.

"Yes, he will," Kurt replied.

Harper left the folded blankets on the seat, stepped to the edge of the carriage and accepted Kurt's hand as she stepped down onto the step, then the ground.

He didn't release her hand, but rather gave it a soft squeeze as he whispered, "It's going to be fine. Trust me."

Trust him? That wasn't possible. She had to trust herself, which, considering the way her arm was heating up from his touch, also felt impossible.

After another soft squeeze to her hand, he gave out a quick, short whistle, and one of Katie Jo's greatest wishes came true as the dog shot down the steps, running toward them.

The next moment was like a reunion of two friends who hadn't seen each other in ages. Katie Jo's arms wrapped around the dog's neck, and he laid his head on her shoulder, as if hugging her in return.

Harper could feel Kurt's gaze on her. Why couldn't she hate him? Why was her entire being thwarting her at every turn? Why did she keep remembering how he used to make her feel, instead of reminding herself that his actions could separate her and Katie Jo forever?

"Grandfather," he said. "This is Katie Jo, and her aunt, Harper Hollister."

Nearly bald and stooped, Axel Cavanaugh offered a broad smile and waved a hand. "Welcome. Come now, let's get you inside where it's warm. I'm sure you're worn out after your travels."

Katie Jo released the dog and moved forward, stopping near the bottom step of the porch. "You're my grandpa," she said, in her tactful way. "My great-grandpa."

"That's right," Axel replied. "I am."

"I've never had a great-grandpa before."

"Well, in all actuality, you have, you just didn't know it," Axel said. "I suspect it'll take us a bit of time to get to know each other."

"What do you want to know?" Katie Jo asked. "I always do my chores, and eat my vegetables. I always do my homework, and I'm an exceptional speller."

Though Axel's eyes were sunken, a sparkle formed as he waved Katie Jo up the steps. "Come. Tell me more."

The subtle pressure of Kurt's hand on the small of her back urged Harper forward, too. She willed her nerves not to get the best of her as she took a step, and then another.

Her footsteps ended on a glossy wooden floor in an eye-catching foyer. The walls were varnished wood, with a massive curved staircase leading to a second floor, and a set of glass doors open to a hallway that led into the main floor of the house. There was also a chandelier overhead, shining brightly with tiny glass electric bulbs.

Katie Jo was in awe over that, and was listening intently as Axel explained that all of the rooms in the house had electric lights and how to turn them on and off with the buttons on the wall.

"You can try out the switches in your room," Kurt said to Katie Jo after the explanation. "It is well past your bedtime." He nodded toward an older woman standing near the staircase. "This is Mrs. Wagner. She will show you and Harper to your bedrooms."

Harper was grateful for his insight and held a hand out to Katie Jo. "Thank you," she said to Kurt, then turned to Axel. "Thank you, Mr. Cavanaugh, for the hospitality."

"You're welcome, Miss Hollister, but please, call me Axel." With a wink to Katie Jo, he added, "Or Grandpa if you prefer."

Katie Jo giggled, but then she frowned slightly as she rubbed Paws behind the ears. "Grandfather, where does Paws sleep?"

Axel looked at the dog, then back at Katie Jo.

"Wherever he falls asleep most nights. Tonight though, I believe he would be honored if you were to allow him to sleep in your room."

Katie Jo gasped, then looked up at Harper.

Harper had no choice but to nod. After bidding both men good-night, she and Katie Jo, and Paws, followed the housekeeper up the curved staircase. The steps were covered with a long, colorful carpet, as was the hallway on the upper floor. Polished wood covered the lower half of the walls, while velvet wallpaper covered the upper half, and electric lights hung at intervals along the ceiling.

Mrs. Wagner eventually stopped and kindly explained that their rooms were across the hall from each other, and that their luggage would be delivered to them directly.

Opening the door, the housekeeper smiled brightly at Katie Jo. "Push that black button right there beside the door. The bottom one."

Katie Jo pushed the button and squealed with delight when an overhead light turned on. "I never hoped about being in a house with electricity, but I should have."

"If you'll follow me for one more minute," Mrs. Wagner said, "I'll show you the water closet. It's at the end of the hall."

Katie Jo shot back out the door with Paws at her side and hurried down the hallway. "This one?"

"Yes, that one," Mrs. Wagner replied.

Katie Jo opened the door and let out a whistle like Harper had never heard before. Then she said, "Lord have mercy!"

"Katie Jo," Harper reprimanded sternly, and offered the housekeeper a look of apology.

Mrs. Wagner had one hand over her mouth, but her eyes were laughing. "Forgive me, miss," the woman whispered. "It's been a long time since there was a child in this house."

"Harper, you have to get in here!" Katie Jo shouted. "You have to see this!"

"I apologize," Harper said. "She's usually very well-behaved."

"Oh, miss, she's just excited, and quite a delight," Mrs. Wagner said. "We've all been looking forward to your visit. I'll go see to your luggage."

Harper could sort their luggage herself, but first needed to see to Katie Jo. She stepped into the room fully prepared to hush her niece, but was too stunned to do more than stare. The room was as large as Kurt's private train car, and all of the necessities, including a huge bathtub, were fully encased in elaborately carved and stained woodwork. There was other furniture too—a large dressing table with a mirror and a tall chest of drawers.

"Have you ever seen anything like this?" Katie Jo asked.

"No, I have not," Harper admitted, with a lump in her throat. Her niece wasn't going to ever want to leave here.

Chapter Seven

Kurt never had trouble sleeping, but did last night. Dreams about Harper kept waking him up. Some had his heart racing with excitement, while others left his heart aching. He wasn't sure which was worse. The one thing he was sure of was that he needed to separate himself from her, at least for a few hours.

But first, he needed to lay down a few rules with his grandfather.

He found the old man in the dining room, dressed for the day in his normal suit and tie, and drinking coffee.

"Oh, good. You're up. How late do you think the little girl will sleep?" his grandfather asked while pointing to a chair.

Kurt sat, accepted a cup of coffee from a kitchen maid and nodded at her silent question, indicating he was ready for breakfast. "Considering it's barely been seven hours since we arrived, I'd suggest you let them sleep as late as they like."

"I planned on that. I was just wondering how long you thought that might be."

Kurt took a swallow of coffee and savored the rich taste for a moment. "I have no idea."

"She looks like Kent, and you," Grandfather said. "She has the Cavanaugh eyes."

"I've noticed that," Kurt replied. "However, need I point out that she knew nothing about us until recently? She's a child, and the only family she knew was Harper."

"I know she's a child. My great-grandchild, and she should have known us long before now."

Kurt met his grandfather's gaze with a solid stare. "Whose fault is that? Not hers. Not Harper's. Not mine."

His grandfather shifted his gaze to the coffee cup in front of him.

That didn't deter Kurt from pointing out the truth. "It's yours. You were the only person who knew, and you chose to keep silent, for years. I want to be perfectly clear." He waited until his grandfather met his gaze again. "I will not allow you to interfere in Katie Jo's life."

"I have not—"

"Yes, you have," Kurt interrupted. "You manipulated Kent until his death and have attempted to manipulate me at nearly every turn. You know that's true, and I know I've allowed it at times. But not this time. That little girl doesn't need you. Not like Kent and I did. She has her aunt, and Harper has done an excellent job of providing for her and raising her without anyone's help. I admire that. You should, too. You should also feel guilty that you were the reason she had to do that all on her own. I certainly do, but I am also grateful for how she has taken care of Katie Jo, and will continue to do so."

"What are you suggesting? That I not have anything to do with my granddaughter? My own flesh and blood?"

His grandfather had mellowed in the past years and had apologized for what he'd done, but Kurt was adamant that he wouldn't fall back into his old habits. "No, you can be her grandfather, but that is all. Your past actions abandoned that little girl for almost seven years, and that alone gives you no right to believe that you can, or attempt to, step in and control her life now."

The maid entered the room, causing his grandfather to hold his comment until after a plate had been set before Kurt and the maid exited.

"You want me to ignore her," Grandfather stated harshly.

"Not at all. During her time here, I expect you to get to know what an amazing child she is, which will not be difficult. She is lovely, and that is owing to her aunt, another thing you need to remember." Kurt picked up his knife and fork. "This is not a business deal, has nothing to do with the railroad. It's a little girl's life, and her aunt's, and ultimately, yours and mine."

His grandfather had never been a quiet man, and his silence now could be concerning. However, it merely made Kurt hold his silence. If it took a stand-off to get his point across, he was more than willing. Acting as if nothing was out of order, he cut a slice off his bacon and ate it.

His plate was nearly empty when his grandfather broke the silence that had grown heavy.

"If you're so dead set against her becoming a Cavanaugh, why did you bring her here?"

Kurt took a drink of coffee. He'd had reservations about this entire thing, still did, but had to admit, his concern centered around Harper. "Katie Jo is a Cavanaugh, has been since birth, conception. What I won't allow is for anyone to give her ultimatums, make her believe that she needs to choose between her aunt and you."

That struck a nerve in his grandfather, because that had always been his main move, to pit two outcomes against each other and sweeten the pot on his side. Shaking his head, his grandfather replied, "At least we agree that she is a Cavanaugh."

Kurt laid his napkin on the table. "If you would get past your own wants, you would see that we agree in other aspects. I'm not expecting miracles, simply for you to see what is in the best interest of Katie Jo." Pushing back his chair, he stood. "Now, if you will excuse me. I have business to attend to this morning. I will return before the noon meal and fully expect you to behave yourself until then."

"Behave myself?"

"Yes, behave yourself." Kurt walked to the doorway and spoke with Lincoln. After asking the butler to inform Harper that he'd return home before noon, Kurt walked to the front door, where Abner was waiting for him, coat in hand and carriage waiting outside.

He had already informed Abner that his first stop would be at the office of his friend, and lawyer, Neil Wyman.

During his on-and-off sleep last night, he'd determined that the best way to assure Harper that she was in no danger of losing guardianship of Katie Jo was to have papers drawn up for her to officially adopt her. After seeing the lawyer, he would assemble a list of qualified tutors and arrange for them to be interviewed by Harper, preferably this afternoon.

Once those tasks were set in motion, he'd be able to get his mind back in order.

It didn't take Harper long to realize one thing. She missed Kurt.

She had never *needed* a man in her life. Not for anything, but deep inside she knew that she wouldn't have felt so vulnerable if he'd been in attendance when she and Katie had entered the dining room, where Axel had sat waiting.

Axel hadn't said or done anything to make her feel uncomfortable. In fact, he was welcoming and friendly, asking about their lives in Pine City in a way that appeared genuine. It was an accumulation of other things. All things. The house was so large and so elegant, it was intimidating. Add in a list of servants ready to respond to a person's every need, and someone like her was bound to be intimidated.

Axel was Katie Jo's grandfather, and had a right to know her. Therefore, Harper kept her fears hidden and a smile on her face as Katie Jo, with her adventurous spirit, embraced everything.

The three of them, Harper, Katie Jo and Axel, were in the lavish front room, with its massive stone fireplace, arched windows that overlooked the Chesapeake Bay and beautifully carved and upholstered furniture with enough seating for two dozen people, when Kurt returned home.

Harper's heart somersaulted in her chest at the sight of him in the doorway, and she had to remind herself that he was the enemy, not the ally that she'd been longing for the past few hours.

Katie Jo, however, had no enemies and instantly leaped to her feet. "Uncle Kurt! You're home! Now we can leave!"

"Leave?" Kurt asked, shooting a frown at his grandfather.

"Not until after lunch," Axel said. Turning to Kurt, he explained, "We've been waiting for Tony to drive us into town."

"Why?" Kurt asked, glancing at Harper.

She could read his mind. He believed she'd convinced Axel to let them return home. If only that was true.

"To go shopping!" Katie Jo rushed forward with the list she'd written and handed it to him. "Harper and Grandpa helped me spell everything correctly."

"Ornaments, red ribbon, silver bells, mistletoe," he said, reading from the very long list.

"Yes! Everything we need to decorate the house for Christmas!" Katie Jo spun around. "Can we eat now? Please?"

Axel stood and held a hand out to Katie Jo. "Let's go see."

"You're going shopping?" Kurt asked, stepping closer to his grandfather.

"Yes, do you object?"

"No," Kurt replied, then stepped aside. "We'll join you in the dining room shortly."

Harper understood Kurt's statement, and the gaze he settled on her. She clasped her hands together to quell how they shook as he approached the green velvet sofa she sat upon.

"He hasn't gone shopping for years," he said.

Not knowing what else to do, Harper shrugged. "When Katie Jo heard that you haven't had a Christmas tree for some time, she created a mission for herself. She saw a picture of a house decorated for Christmas in a catalog a few weeks ago and is set upon re-creating it."

He chuckled. "The list she made should do that."

"I will try to keep it in check," she said.

He sat in the chair opposite her. "I don't believe anyone will be able to keep that list in check, but would you be opposed to having Abner accompany them instead of you? I can guarantee he will keep a close eye on her, and grandfather."

"Why don't you want me to go?"

"It's not that I don't want you to go, it's because I have set up appointments for you this afternoon."

"What sort of appointments?"

"Interviews for a tutor. Seven of them. They will begin to arrive at one-thirty. It's part of her care, which I agreed you'd have the final say in, so I'd like you to be the one to make the decision on the tutor. We agreed she wouldn't fall behind on her studies."

Yes, she had agreed to that, but allowing Katie Jo to go without her was a concern.

"If it would make you feel more comfortable, I can ask Mrs. Wagner to accompany them as well," he said.

If all of this was going to teach her anything, it was that she'd have to learn to share Katie Jo. The life they had known was over, and the quicker she accepted that, the better off she'd be. Then she could focus on what she could do, rather than what she couldn't. She knew she couldn't fight the Cavanaughs, so she'd best figure out a way to work with them. "All right, but I'd like to talk to Katie Jo about it first."

"Of course," Kurt replied.

He knew exactly what she knew, that Katie Jo would agree. After gobbling down her food in record time, she ran to collect her outerwear.

"Now, you be good," Harper said, while kneeling down and buttoning Katie Jo's coat, even though she'd been able to do that by herself for years. "And keep your mittens on."

"I will. I promise." Katie Jo then wrapped her arms around Harper's neck. "Aren't you glad that Uncle Kurt found us? I sure am. So glad that when I look at him, my heart beats faster. Not like when I see a spider or something scary, but like when I see a puppy. Like Paws. He sure is a nice dog."

The dog seemed to be as enthralled with Katie Jo as she was him. He'd barely left her side since their arrival last night. "Yes, he is a nice dog," Harper replied.

Katie Jo stepped back. "You're glad Uncle Kurt found us, too, aren't you?"

Harper would never be able to admit that, so she kissed Katie Jo's forehead and said, "I'm glad you're happy."

Katie Jo frowned. "Doesn't Uncle Kurt make your heart beat faster?"

Unable to lie, Harper avoided answering the question by giving Katie Jo a playful tickling before taking a hold of her hand. "We don't want everyone waiting on you, and you must promise me that you'll tell me all about the stores you visit." That was a given, but a change of subject that Katie Jo would quickly accept.

"I will, and I hope you find me a teacher as nice as Miss Carpenter."

"I will try my hardest," Harper agreed.

Moments later, as the carriage pulled away from the house, with Katie Jo tucked up against Axel's side and waving excitedly, Kurt took a hold of Harper's elbow to escort her back into the house.

"Don't worry, she'll be fine."

"Have you ever gone shopping with a six-year-old?" she asked.

"No."

"Then you don't understand that it's the others with her that I'm worried about."

He chuckled. "They won't lose their patience with her. She's already endeared herself to all of them. Both Abner and Mrs. Wagner eagerly agreed to the task." He opened the house door. "The interviews will be conducted in the library, and there's just enough time to go over the list of names and their qualifications prior to the first one arriving."

Harper hadn't realized he'd planned on partaking in the interviews until the first woman arrived, and then she was quite grateful. Miss Plumberger was significantly qualified, but Harper couldn't get past the woman's hawkish face and beady eyes.

"Thank you for making yourself available today," Kurt said, after he'd asked a variety of questions, then rose to his feet. "We will be making a decision later today and will send out messages to all applicants this evening."

Miss Plumberger gave a slight nod as she stood from where the three of them were seated at an oval table in the library and leveled a steely glare, which made Harper quiver.

"I would like to reiterate that I have never had a behavior issue with any of my students," Miss Plumberger said.

"We will make note of that," Kurt replied, already at the door. "Thank you again for coming, Miss Plumberger. Mr. Ford will see you out to your carriage." As soon as the woman had exited, he closed the door. "Behavior issues," he whispered. "That woman would make the devil toe the line with one of her glares."

Harper let out a sigh of relief.

Back at the table, Kurt sat in his chair next to her and drew a line through Miss Plumberger's name. "We agree she's not a possibility?"

"Yes," Harper agreed wholeheartedly.

She barely said a word during the next interview either, which was with a very pretty woman who barely took her eyes off Kurt. Every one of her answers was full of batting eyelashes and annoying giggles.

Upon that woman's exit, Harper was surprised

when Kurt once again crossed a name off the list with a single stroke of his pencil.

Shaking his head, he said, "On to the next."

Mrs. Agate was an elderly widow, with rosy cheeks and twinkling blue eyes, who spoke loudly, asking about Katie Jo. But she also referred to Harper as Mrs. Cavanaugh, even though it had been made clear that she and Kurt were Katie Jo's aunt and uncle, not parents, and that they were not married.

When she left, and Kurt sat down, he put a question mark next to Mrs. Agate's name. "Do you think Katie Jo would like her?"

Harper shrugged. "She adores Miss Carpenter, who is, well, younger and full of energy." Feeling guilty over her comment, she quickly added, "But a tutor with one child is different from a classroom full of children."

"That is true, and we'll all be able hear her lessons."

The shine in his eyes had her pinching her lips together.

His grin grew. "You know that's the truth. It's all right to laugh once in a while."

She shook her head. "Not at the expense of someone else."

He nodded. "Note taken. The next one is…"

Harper's heart sank. She hadn't meant to sound

so harsh, she just couldn't get too comfortable, and that's how he made her feel. Comfortable, when she shouldn't be. Yet, she had agreed to do this with him and did appreciate his insightfulness. "I'm sorry."

He'd stopped reading aloud.

"I know you weren't being mean," she added quickly.

"I wasn't." He brushed a strand of hair away from the side of her face and looked at her tenderly. "I just wanted to make you laugh."

The draw she felt inside her was so strong it locked her breathing, and she couldn't keep her eyes from bouncing between his lips and eyes. Her heart stopped as he leaned closer, and her lips tingled with anticipation.

"You don't laugh often enough," he said softly.

She twisted her face away, embarrassed that she'd wanted him to kiss her. Wanted it so badly. "I live with Katie Jo. I laugh a lot."

He chuckled. "She is very amusing."

The next three applicants, two men and one woman, were not options in Harper's mind for various reasons, and all it took was one shared look with Kurt to know that he agreed.

"I had no idea how difficult this would be," Harper said.

"Perhaps you or I could be her tutor. Or Grandpa."

She laughed. "The two of them would do nothing but play with the toy train he showed her today."

"Did he put oil in the smokestack? To make it smoke?"

"Yes," she answered. "Several times."

A knock sounded on the door, and he stood. "He loves that train."

Judging from the smile on his face, she said, "I think you do, too."

He winked at her. "It's inherited."

She told her heart to settle down, but it didn't listen.

Chapter Eight

As Kurt made his way to the door, the smile on his face never faded. He did love that train, but he was thoroughly enjoying completing this task with Harper. It was easy to read her mind, and fun to watch her thoughts cross her face. Even though he'd caught himself within seconds of kissing her.

At least that had proven he had some control left. He was going to need it, that was for sure.

He opened the door and greeted the last applicant, Mrs. Gallagher. She was young, nice and very interested in learning more about Katie Jo. She'd resigned from teaching after getting married a few months ago and missed her students.

Kurt barely spoke during the interview. The two women talked as if they were long-lost friends. He was touched by how much it meant to see Harper happy and at ease. There were other thoughts floating in his mind, too. For the first time he could ever remember, he was wondering about children, wondering if Harper wanted children. More than Katie Jo.

When Harper glanced his way with a full smile on her face, he smiled back and gave her a slight nod in agreement that Mrs. Gallagher was the perfect choice. "When would you be able to start, Mrs. Gallagher?" he asked.

"Tomorrow?" she answered. "My husband is an engineer for the city passenger rail, so I'm available all day, but would like to be home by six, if possible."

"That's completely possible," he replied. "We have concluded that a few hours each morning will be all that Katie Jo requires, between now and Christmas." After going over a few other logistics, the woman left, agreeing to return the next morning.

He turned to Harper. "Satisfied?"

"Very." She leaned forward and propped her chin on her fist. "What is the city passenger rail?"

He wasn't ready for their time together to be over, and walked toward the table. "Baltimore has been known as the city of firsts for years. Being the first major port, it was the first city to be declared as the gateway to the West. It gave birth to the first National roadway, the first railroad, and the first telegraph was sent from the train station here. Now this year, it's the first city to host an electric trolly—trams that travel on rails to and from the busiest parts of the city."

"Do you own it?"

"The East Central Railroad owns the trams. The city owns the tracks. They used horse-drawn trams on them for years."

"The men who work on the trams work for you?"

"Yes." He sat down next to her and felt a great need to explain, "There is nothing I can do about the past, but I assure you, in the future, I will not let my family or the railroad cause you pain. I know your father—"

Shaking her head, she held up a hand. "My father never complained about working at the railyard. I never heard him say a bad thing about it, and when he died, it was Mr. Mason, his boss, who said that if Sherri or I were to get a job at the restaurant, we could continue to live in the house. We were grateful for that."

Her long lashes fluttered shut for a moment, and he had to fight the urge to just take her hand in comfort.

"It wasn't until—" She shook her head. "It wasn't your fault, and you have every right to be proud of the tram system. Of Baltimore and all of its firsts, including the East Central Railroad. I asked only because of Katie Jo. If there are railcars that she can ride on downtown, they may never convince her to come back."

"I hadn't thought of that," he said, feeling a sense of relief.

"I did."

"Well, the trams end at six," he said.

She let out a small huff. "If the men who drive the trams work for your grandfather, he may tell them to keep on driving."

Kurt rubbed his chin in order to hide a slight chuckle. She could very well be right. Furthermore, in a very short time, she'd figured his grandfather out to a T. "Do you want to go and look for them?"

"They took the carriage."

He stood. "We have more than one carriage, and more than one person who can drive them. Tony is just Grandfather's favorite." He grinned. "Believe it or not, I can drive a team of horses myself."

She was so pretty when she smiled. Her dark brown eyes glimmered as if filled with stars, and her face took on a shine of its own. He remembered that from years ago, and it had the ability to take his breath away. If he had a wish, or a hope as Katie Jo called them, it would be to see Harper smiling and laughing all the time.

"I believe you," she said. "And no, we don't need to go and look for them. Yet."

The problem with a face that pretty, and a personality that plucky, was that it might make him lose his good sense.

"I believe we have some messages to write," she said. "To those who we aren't going to hire."

He was more than willing to remain in her company, and crossed the room to collect stationery from the desk drawer. As they wrote, they discussed the city tram, and soon he was telling her about his vision of seeing trams in all of the major eastern cities, and beyond. He also explained how he saw an automobile revolution on the horizon. She asked thoughtful questions that continued their conversation long after the notes had been written.

In fact, they stayed in the library, talking about many topics, until the door flew open and a rosy-cheeked Katie Jo exclaimed, "You have to see all the things we bought!"

Long after she tucked Katie Jo into bed across the hall, Harper remained awake, lying in bed with visions flashing in her head. They weren't images of the Christmas trees, red ribbons or silver bells Katie Jo had talked nonstop about all evening.

They were all images of Kurt. She kept telling herself that she needed to hate him, to consider him the enemy, to stay away from him, but none of that was what she wanted. Not deep down, where it really mattered. In fact, she was beginning to accept that she had no real reason to hate him, no reason to consider him the enemy. And, like Katie Jo, her heart beat faster at the sight of him.

It had done that years ago, too, and though she still didn't believe in love at first sight, she had never wanted someone to kiss her before either, not like she did today.

Conducting the interviews and talking with him for the rest of the afternoon had been so wonderful, so special. She was busy back home, working at the store and, though the Johnsons were always near and she had friends, none of that addressed the loneliness inside of her. During the hours she'd spent with Kurt today, that had gone away. Completely. It hadn't returned until she lay down and the day had replayed in her mind.

Guilt grew inside her. She had Katie Jo and loved her dearly, so she shouldn't ever feel lonely.

Other images formed, those of Axel, how from the moment they'd entered the dining room, he'd doted upon Katie Jo. It was more than that; Katie Jo had also been instantly taken with him. Had her niece been lonely inside, too? Longing to have others in their lives? A family?

Come morning, Harper couldn't remember when she'd finally fallen asleep, but knew the moment she woke up. It was when Katie Jo, already dressed, landed on her bed, quickly followed by Paws.

"Time to get up! It's decorating day!" Plopping on her bottom, Katie Jo clasped her hands together and held them beneath her chin. "This is the best Christmas ever! The best! Don't you think?"

In her niece's eyes it was, therefore Harper agreed, "Yes, it is."

After a hug and a quick bout of tickling, Harper climbed out of bed and, following Katie Jo's requests to hurry, they were soon in the dining room, having breakfast with Axel and Kurt. The discussion was solely on the decorating that would take place that day.

Even a reminder that her new tutor would be there for a few hours that morning didn't suppress Katie Jo's enthusiasm. The only person who appeared put out was Axel, who claimed he could have been her tutor. His comment caused Harper to look at Kurt, and they both laughed.

Neither Axel or Katie saw the humor.

That created a pattern for the next couple of days. Mrs. Gallagher in the mornings and decorating in the afternoons and evenings, until every room had been decked. Harper had to agree with Katie Jo that the house was even more beautiful than the picture in the magazine.

As soon as breakfast was over on Saturday morning, Axel announced it was time for everyone to get their coats.

"May I ask why?" Kurt inquired while giving Harper a glance.

She shrugged and looked at Axel for his answer.

"Because the toboggan we bought the other day was delivered yesterday," he said. "It's time to try it out."

"Hold on," Kurt said. "Let's think about this. You—"

"I'm not going to ride on it," Axel said. "I'll watch the three of you. It snowed again last night, so this morning is perfect for tobogganing."

Harper had her concerns about sliding down a hill that led to the bay, but she was outnumbered. Soon, bundled as warmly as possible, they were outside, at the top of the hill, with the toboggan near Harper's feet.

"We'll stop before getting near the water," Kurt said. "Climb on."

"Are you sure?"

"Very," he said. "Trust me."

She looked at the dark, icy-looking water. "In this case, that is easier said than done."

He laughed.

"Come on, Harper!" Katie Jo was already seated at the front of the toboggan, where the long, narrow wooden slats curled up in a hook shape. "You have to sit like this," she said. "With your legs crossed and hold on to the rope loops on the sides."

Harper gave Kurt one last look, and then, following instructions, settled herself onto the wood, carefully tucking her skirt beneath her to keep it from getting too wet. Her breath caught as Kurt sat down close behind her. She wasn't convinced this was safe, but if there was anyone she could trust, it would be him.

"Ready?" he asked.

"Yes!" answered Katie Jo.

Harper remained silent and tightened her hold on the rope loops.

They started out slow, with Kurt pushing them forward with his hands, but as soon as the front of the long toboggan slipped over the edge of the hill, the rest swiftly followed. The trip down the hill was fast, and to Harper's surprise, she heard her own laugh amongst Kurt's deep one and Katie Jo's excited squeals. It was fun, thrilling, and filled her with a joy she hadn't felt in a long time.

Kurt's arms had come around her as soon as the ride down the hill had started because he was using the large loop of rope that came up from beneath the curved hook to steer the toboggan. They stopped at the bottom of the hill, far from the water because he'd expertly turned the long sled to one side and brought it to a smooth stop.

Katie Jo's laughter surrounded them, along with Paws's barking.

Harper glanced over her shoulder at Kurt. "You've done this before."

"Many times," he said. "Kent and I used to spend hours racing each other down the hill."

Leaping off the toboggan, Katie Jo asked, "Can we do it again?"

"Absolutely." Kurt climbed off and helped Harper stand. "The only downside is pulling the toboggan back up the hill."

Katie Jo and Paws were already running up the hill, where Axel was sitting in a chair.

No longer worried about the hem of her skirt getting snow soaked, Harper took hold of the rope to help Kurt pull it up the hill. "Did your grandpa sit and watch you and Kent do this?"

Kurt laughed. "Most of the time, he was riding with us. I think he loved it as much as we did. There are several old toboggans in the rafters of the stable, but they need to be soaked and waxed, having dried out years ago."

Harper frowned, wondering why she'd thought that Axel had been a mean man who'd sat behind his desk, yelling at people to work harder, make him more money. As she'd told Kurt, her father had never said a bad word about the railroad. The first time she'd heard awful tales about the Cavanaugh family had been when she'd started working at the restaurant, and it had all come from other waitresses who had failed to catch the attention of Kurt or Kent, despite their continued attempts.

Yet, it had taken root. She'd listened and believed and had gained proof when Kent had married a blue blood instead of her sister.

"Yippie!" Katie Jo hopped onto the toboggan as soon as they topped the hill and turned it around. "Come on, Harper! Get on!"

Katie Jo had never looked happier, and that filled Harper's heart. She sat down on the toboggan, tucked her skirts beneath her, and this time, she let all of her fears and worries go and enjoyed the swift slide down the snowy slope.

It was even more fun than the first trip. So were the ones that followed, until Paws, during his race down the hill beside them, shot in front of their path. Kurt quickly steered the toboggan to keep from hitting the dog, but the change of direction flipped the sled and tossed them into the snow.

Harper wasn't sure how he'd done it, but when their tumbling ended, Kurt had one arm locked around her and the other around Katie Jo. Both of them were partly lying on his chest and he was flat on his back in the snow.

"Everyone all right?" he asked.

"Yes!" Katie Jo replied. "That was so fun!"

"Harper?" he asked.

Her face burned. All she could think about was her body touching his, and how there wasn't a part of her that wanted to move. Until a sense of panic struck and she scrambled to get off of him. She managed to push her torso upward, but her skirt was caught underneath his legs, trapping her legs against one of his. The heat that raced through her entire being was flaming hot.

He was looking at her in a deep, penetrating way. To add to her horror, her lips were tingling again at the thought of him kissing her. He was thinking the same thing, she was sure of it, and she couldn't look away. Couldn't stop wanting.

"Look!" Katie Jo shouted. "Paws is pulling the to-boggan!"

The spell was broken and, after some untangling, from both her and Kurt, they sat up enough to look down the hill and see the dog with the rope in his mouth, heading uphill.

"Good," Kurt said. "From now on he can ride down the hill, too. That'll keep him out of our way."

Harper wondered if he was as flustered as she was. Her body was trembling, and it wasn't from the cold.

"Are you all right?" Kurt asked.

"Yes," Harper replied, even though her body was still reacting in ways it never had before. She accepted his help off the ground, and once they topped the hill, she declined another trek down on the toboggan.

With Paws now sitting in the front of the toboggan, then Katie Jo, and then Kurt, they took off down the hill again, with much laughter and barking.

"Have a seat," Axel said. "It's quite a show to watch."

Harper sat in one of the wooden lawn chairs arranged at the top of the hill and focused on getting her thoughts and body back in check as she watched the toboggan make it all the way to the bottom without a mishap.

As they started back up the hill, Kurt was coaxing Paws to pull the sled. The dog would do so for a few steps and then drop the rope. Kurt would pull for a few steps, then drop the rope and tell Paws to pick it up. The dog would, and pulled it for another few steps. It was making the trek slow, but Katie Jo didn't seem to mind. She was copying Kurt as he praised the dog.

"Mark my word," Axel said. "Kurt will have that

dog pulling the toboggan up the hill by himself before the day's end."

"He might at that," Harper agreed.

"He's good at that," Axel said. "Teaching. He doesn't tell people what to do, he shows them."

Harper couldn't agree with that. Kurt had told her she and Katie Jo were coming with him point-blank. However, for whatever reason, she was no longer angry about that.

"A man doesn't live to be my age without acquiring regrets." Axel let out a deep sigh. "I'm no different. There are things I wish I'd done differently. Putting the business first all of the time is one of them. I did wrong by Kent. Did wrong by that little girl right there, and I did wrong by your sister. I thought my reasons were good. Thought I knew the kind of woman he should marry, promised her father they would wed, but I was wrong. So wrong."

Harper had no reply, simply looked at his face, at the sincerity in his sunken, aged eyes, and felt a wave of empathy. For him, and perhaps for herself.

Axel shook his head. "I'll never be able to repay you for letting me have this time with Katie Jo, and I'll never forget it."

She was saved from having to respond by Katie Jo topping the hill and rushing forward.

"Look, Grandpa! Uncle Kurt is teaching Paws to pull the toboggan up the hill."

"I see that." Axel lifted Katie Jo onto his lap, as snow covered as she was. "Maybe I'll have to buy the two of you one of those dogsleds like they have up in Alaska, so he can pull you around the yard. Wouldn't that be something?"

"It sure would!" Katie Jo hugged him.

"I think he needs to master the toboggan first." Kurt dropped the rope that he'd been pulling the last few feet and sat down in the chair next to hers. "But I'm glad to see it's rest time." Looking at her, he asked, "No worse for wear?"

"No," she answered. It was a lie.

Chapter Nine

He wasn't old, had only hit his twenty-ninth birthday last fall, yet parts of Kurt hurt like he was as aged as his grandfather. Who knew tobogganing could be so hard on a person?

Sinking deeper into the hot water in the bathtub, he let out a long sigh. It had been fun and, given the opportunity, he'd repeat the entire morning. Especially the part when he and Harper had ended up legs entangled. He'd never wanted to kiss someone so badly in his life as he had at that moment.

If the opportunity occurred again, he might take advantage of it. He wanted to, that was for damn sure.

He shook his head. What the hell was wrong with him? He couldn't do that. That wouldn't be fair to her. He was cursed. That hadn't changed. Would never change. Love and marriage brought nothing but loss.

He wished that Neil was in town. The lawyer had gone to New York and wouldn't be back until next week. Due to the circumstances, he didn't want anyone else drawing up the adoption paperwork, so he'd have to wait.

He could tell Harper about the adoption, but he wanted the paperwork in hand when he did, to show her that he'd never take Katie Jo away from her.

A knock sounded on the door of his private suite, and Kurt sat up, resting his arms along the edge of the bathtub in readiness for Abner to deliver the glass of whiskey he'd ordered to help take the sting out of his muscles. "Come in!" At the sound of the door opening, he added, "In here!"

A moment later, when it was Harper who appeared in the doorway, he startled at being caught in the tub. There were suds, but not that many! He quickly grabbed the washcloth and dropped it over his groin. It didn't cover much, but would have to do.

Or so he thought, until she spun around and bolted away from the door.

"Harper!" He pushed himself upright. "Wait! What's wrong?"

"Wrong?" Her shout filtered through the room. "You could have said you were in the tub!"

"I thought you were Abner!" Out of the tub now, he grabbed a larger towel. Wrapping it around his waist, he hurried toward the door. "Why are you here?"

"I wanted to talk to you, but it can wait."

"You're here, so…" He let his words fade as he crossed into his drawing room. She'd stopped halfway across the room because Abner stood in the open doorway with a tray in hand.

She spun around, and her eyes widened at his towel attire before she made a half turn, so she wasn't facing either him or Abner.

Kurt walked to the door, took the tray. "Thank you. That will be all for now."

"Yes, sir." Abner closed the door as he left.

"Drink?" Kurt asked her.

"No!" Her shoulders lifted as she drew in a breath. "Thank you." Her voice went softer as she asked, "He won't tell anyone, will he?"

"No, Abner won't tell anyone." He set the tray on the table. "What was it you wanted to talk to me about? I thought you and Katie Jo were going to take baths to warm up, too."

She let out another sigh, but still didn't turn around. "Katie Jo is taking a bath. I will take one when she's done. I wanted to ask you about all of the new clothes in my room."

"New clothes?" He walked to his bedroom to collect his robe from the wardrobe. "I don't know anything about new clothes."

"Yes, you do. My room is full of them. So is Katie Jo's. Dresses, shoes, coats, under—everything. Gifts for Katie Jo is one thing, but I draw the line at having you buy anything for me."

He shrugged on his robe and tied it while walking back into the drawing room. "I didn't buy any new clothes. Not for you or Katie Jo. Maybe Katie Jo picked them out when she and Grandpa went shopping." Things they'd bought continued to be delivered every day.

"No. I asked her."

He stopped in front of her and lifted her chin, so she had to look at him, rather than the floor. "Then it must have been Grandpa."

"I can't accept gifts from him, either." She closed her eyes. "I know our clothes aren't as elegant—"

"There is nothing wrong with your clothes," he interrupted. "Or with Katie Jo's. Grandpa would have bought them just to do something nice for you. He appreciates what you've done."

She opened her eyes, stared at him. "There's nothing to appreciate. She's my niece."

He grasped her upper arms. "She's also his great-granddaughter. It might be misguided, but he's trying to make up for what he did to Kent and Sherri. Trying to right a wrong."

"Clothes won't make us fit into this world. Nothing will." She stepped backward, breaking the hold he had on her arms. "I won't be steamrolled into thinking this will be the best place for Katie Jo. It won't be."

"I've never said this would be the best place for Katie Jo."

"You want her to see how luxurious life is here. How all her hopes can come true here. Including a dog!"

"Paws has been here for years."

"That's not the point. You don't want your life to change! Well, we don't, either. Can't you understand that?"

"It's already changed, Harper. Whether we wanted it to or not. It will continue to, and the truth is, I don't mind."

"Our life is in Pine City. Everyone Katie Jo knows lives there."

His chest tightened. He hadn't been thinking solely of Katie Jo. Still wasn't, and he wondered if that's why she was so upset. "I saw the life she had there, saw how much she enjoyed it, but you're wrong. Everyone she *had* known lives there. Now she knows people who live here, too. I'm still not saying this is the best place for her, so don't put words in my mouth. I don't care where she lives, because I will see her, and so will Grandpa. If that means traveling to Pine City, so be it. Even after you marry and start your own family."

The chill that instantly hit the room was colder than it had been outside. He hadn't meant to say that aloud. She just got to him, in so many ways.

Her mouth was open, her eyes wide. "Marry?"

He'd gone this far, might as well get it over with. "Yes. Every woman wants to get married."

Her expression went from angry to sad. Of all the times he had been able to read her mind, this wasn't one of them, and he wished like hell that it was.

"Not when their heart has already been broken."

She turned to leave and he grasped her hand. He wanted to know who had broken her heart. More than that, he wanted to help her heal it.

He had no idea how to do that, and glanced upward instinctually, for help or divine inspiration. The electric chandelier was all he saw. The one that had a sprig of mistletoe hanging from it. Katie Jo's decorating had hit every room, and declining red ribbons and silver bells, he'd agreed to the sprig.

His gaze returned to Harper. Her eyes were closed, her fingers beneath his were trembling, and he wanted to kiss her more than ever. Not doing so was an agony he'd never known. Every part of him was throbbing, telling him to kiss her. Even his self-control had deserted him.

It had snapped. He'd felt it vibrate through his entire being a moment ago. That mistletoe was a sign, a way to show her that even broken hearts could be healed.

In one swift movement, he pulled her up against him, and his lips captured hers.

She gasped, and the temptation that he'd been fighting sought full control.

There was but a single ounce of common sense left inside him, and it was on the brink of telling him to release her, apologize, when she moved.

A soft little cooing sound echoed in his ears as her body went from frozen to warm, and her soft, perfect curves melded against him as her arms went around his neck.

His kiss became heated and full of emotion. One that said not kissing her would have been the death of him, because that was exactly how he felt.

Her lips danced beneath his, like a game of catch me if you can.

He could, and did. Over and over again.

Still needing more, he ran his tongue along the seam of her lips, and when they parted, he entered her mouth. Kissed her so thoroughly his heart hammered inside his chest.

This was the last thing Harper had expected. The very last thing. Then why didn't she want it to stop? Why was she clinging to him like she was drowning and he was the only one who could save her? She'd dreamed of kissing him. For years. Both asleep and awake, and yet it was far better than her meager mind had ever imagined.

Nothing had ever been this thrilling. This consuming. He tasted so good. His body felt so amazing, all firm and muscular, and his hair, where her fingers were buried in the back of his head, was like silk, and slightly damp.

Probably from the bath she'd interrupted.

She'd never been so horrified in her life.

But would do it again, considering this was the result.

A little moan rumbled in her throat, and she stretched higher on her toes, giving in to the urgent need that was driving her every move. His arms wrapped around her, providing a world she'd never known.

All thoughts left her as the sensations of kissing him, of pressing against him, became her only focus.

He was the one to slowly end the kiss, sweetly, with soft little pecks on her lips, before he completely lifted his head and looked down at her.

For a moment, she was engulfed in a wonderful fog, then a faint feeling that she should turn and run away crept in. But she couldn't. Her legs were rubbery.

She had to do something.

Anything.

Slowly, she withdrew her hands from his hair, slipped her arms off his shoulders.

He sighed softly and, sensing that he was going to say something, she pressed a finger to his lips and shook her head.

Her face felt flushed, her lips swollen. She bit the tip of her tongue, still tasting him, and told herself that at times, silence was the best option. So was leaving.

When her sanity returned, she would know what to do. Know what to think about all of this.

She took a step back, withdrew her finger from his lips as his hands released the hold he had on her hips. There was a great battle inside her, because she knew she was about to walk away from the one thing she'd always wanted, would always want. But it was also the one thing she feared beyond all else. Loving a Cavanaugh.

He had already broken her heart once. That was a realization she'd only come to moments ago, when he'd mentioned marriage. For years, she'd told herself that she'd never marry because of Katie Jo, but that had been a lie. *He* was the reason. It was foolish, because he'd barely known she was alive all those years ago, but she'd been in love with him.

She turned and begged her legs not to fail her as she walked to the door.

"Harper."

Acting as if she hadn't heard, she kept walking, opened the door and closed it behind her. The click vibrated through her, and at that moment—that stilled, silent moment standing in the hallway—she knew one thing for sure. She would carry an invisible mark of him on her heart for the rest of her life.

It shouldn't come as a surprise. It had already been there. She could just no longer ignore it. Nor could she ignore how she'd waited, hoped, that he'd find her after she'd quit working at the depot. It had been childish to want a knight in shining armor to come to her rescue, but that's what she'd dreamed of. Right up until Katie Jo had been born, when she realized that if he did show up, it would be to take Katie Jo away from her.

She took her time walking through the house, so large that if a person on one end yelled, those on the other wouldn't even hear an echo. It wasn't the house's fault that it was big and beautiful. It wasn't Kurt's, either. She couldn't even blame Axel. Nor could she blame them for wanting Katie Jo to have more than she could ever give her.

By the time Harper reached her room, she was no

longer trembling, no longer breathing in short gasps, not that either helped much.

The wardrobe door was still open, the way she'd left it upon seeing how it had been filled with various garments while they were sledding. More garments than she'd owned collectively since birth. She was sure of that.

"There you are!" Katie Jo said, bursting into the room. "I finished my bath, brushed my hair and got dressed, but the buttons are in the back."

Since the day Katie Jo had been born, Harper had put aside all her own wants and dreams to focus on her niece. That's how it had to be and would continue to be. She pulled up a smile and knelt down. "Well, then, let me help you."

Katie Jo spun around, exposing the row of undone buttons on the back of the dark green, white lace-encrusted dress. "Where were you?" Katie Jo asked, "I looked in here and my room."

"She was talking to me."

Harper's fingers shook at the sound of Kurt's voice. Shocked, she twisted to look at him, half expecting to see him wearing just his robe again. Having seen his bare, muscular chest, arms, rib cage, thighs, knees, feet…she'd never be able to unsee them. Even when he was dressed.

Which he was now. Fully. In black pants and a

white shirt, with thin black suspenders over his shoulders.

"That must be one of your new dresses," he said to Katie Jo. "It's very pretty."

"I know," Katie Jo replied, beaming brightly.

Harper cleared her throat slightly.

"Thank you," Katie Jo added.

"All done," Harper said, giving Katie Jo's long hair a gentle hand smoothing.

"Can I go downstairs and show Grandpa?"

Harper didn't want to be alone with Kurt. "Yes, I will walk you down."

"I'm not a baby. I can go by myself. You can take your bath now. Or talk to Uncle Kurt again."

Chapter Ten

Harper watched as her niece shot past Kurt, who was still standing in the doorway, and wished, truly wished, that she had some defense against him.

"I'm sorry," he said quietly. "I can't leave things like this."

Yes, he could, because it would give her time to figure out what to do.

"I won't apologize for kissing you," he said. "That was something I've wanted to do for a long time. But I will apologize for not asking your permission." He leaned one hand against the door frame. "I know coming here wasn't what you wanted, or what you wanted for Katie Jo."

She wasn't ready for a conversation about kissing him, nor to contemplate him wanting to kiss her, even as her heart started thudding. So, instead, she said, "I don't want Katie Jo to get hurt. She depends on me for that."

"She depends on you for a lot of things," he said. "But who do you depend on?"

Taken aback by the question, she shook her head. "Myself."

"Why?"

"Because there is no one else."

"Why is that?" he asked, stepping closer.

She took a step back while trying to come up with an answer. "Because..." His expectant expression had her repeating, "There is no one else."

"Yes, there is." He stopped near a chair, rested a hand on the back of it. "I've always been here and, had you asked, would have helped from the beginning."

Harper rubbed her arms at the chill rippling over her. "I couldn't do that."

"Because you were afraid."

It was more important than ever that she kept her wits about her. "Because I had a baby to take care of. Katie Jo was, and will always be, my first concern. Now, if you will excuse me, I'd like to change my clothes so she can have her lunch."

"Harper—"

"You've never seen a child hungry, have you?" She took a dress, one of her old ones, out of the closet and walked toward the door. "They can become quite unmanageable."

She left the room and walked to the water closet, thankful that he didn't follow.

Her thoughts and emotions were what had become unmanageable, and she had to do something about them.

That was going to take time after the kiss she'd shared with Kurt, and she was glad, yet woeful, when he wasn't present for lunch. She'd admitted to herself what was at the very root of her fears, but still didn't know what to do about it.

Kurt had returned home for dinner, and she did her best to act as if all was fine.

She did the same the following morning, too, when she put on one of the new dresses that Axel had purchased for her.

"You sure do look pretty, Harper," Katie Jo declared as they walked hand in hand to the breakfast table.

"I agree," Kurt said, holding a chair out for her.

"Me, too," Axel said, smiling at Harper. "I had Mrs. Wagner determine your size and was hoping the new clothes would fit. Were you surprised to see them?"

"Yes, I was," Harper replied, feeling heat in her cheeks at the memory of what she'd done, and seen, after finding the dresses in her closet. "Thank you very much."

"A thousand dresses couldn't come close to repaying you for what you've done," Axel said. "You've made me the happiest old man in the state." He looked at Katie Jo, who had taken her usual chair beside his. "Make that the whole world."

"I'm happy, too!" Katie Jo agreed. "After church we're making gingerbread houses! I'm going to use only red gumdrops on my house."

"That might make the other gumdrops sad," Axel said.

Katie Jo frowned. "I hadn't thought of that. Maybe I'll use all of the colors, but only eat the red ones, because they are my favorite."

Axel agreed that was a good plan, and gingerbread houses continued to dominate the conversation as they ate, including how shocked Katie Jo was to hear that Kurt had never made one.

After breakfast, they traveled in the carriage to a church downtown. Baltimore was not only the city of firsts, it was the city of the biggest and the best. That was also true of the massive church. The stained glass windows covered one entire wall and shrouded the sanctuary with a rainbow of brilliant shards of light.

The four of them walked to their seats, with Axel and Katie Jo leading the way. People already seated smiled and nodded as they approached, but she could feel their eyes still on them after they'd passed by and taken their seats.

She and Katie Jo sat side by side, flanked by Axel and Kurt. Harper gently straightened Katie Jo's flat brimmed black hat, as well as the long white ribbons that hung down off the back, while hoping her own flowered hat that matched the layered, olive-colored gown, was still positioned correctly. Kurt had assisted her in removing her coat upon entrance to the church and had carried it, along with his own, over his arm.

To say she'd been nervous about attending the church service was putting it mildly, and even now her hands shook.

Whether he noticed that, or simply knew, Kurt laid a hand over her clasped ones and gave her a soft smile. In spite of all she knew about herself, his touch was comforting.

Since their kiss, she'd thought of little else, and had to admit something to herself. He hadn't broken her heart. She'd done that herself by putting expectations on him that he'd never known anything about. The other hard fact that she'd had to accept was that she'd never fallen out of love with him.

The service was reverent, fixed on the season and was over before Katie Jo grew restless. They put on their coats and left their pew, as the group of people mingling near the doorway seemed to be gathering with intent.

Her chin trembled slightly, wondering if this, attending church with Kurt and Axel, would bring about her worst nightmare—for people to single out Katie Jo.

Kurt's hand was hooked around one of her elbows as they walked behind Axel and Katie Jo. Both men greeted people, but despite the churchgoers clearly wanting to know more, neither paused long enough for that to happen.

They exited the building and climbed into the carriage, and as they pulled away, Axel let out a laugh.

"What are you laughing about, Grandpa?" Katie Jo asked.

"I'm just happy," he said. "A man my age doesn't get the opportunity to pull the wool over someone's eyes all that often."

Katie Jo frowned. "I didn't see you touch anyone's hat."

Harper shared an amused look with Kurt.

"They were invisible hats," Axel said, winking at her and Kurt. "Half the people back there were scratching their heads, but they know me well enough not to ask questions, because they won't get any answers."

Harper couldn't help but wonder if, rather than

pulling the wool over anyone's eyes, their attendance had just given wings to the gossip.

Kurt declined an invitation to decorate gingerbread houses, stating he had something to do. Which was true. He had a lot of thinking to do. Kissing Harper in his bedroom yesterday had created quite a dilemma. It had satisfied a craving, while also making it worse.

He'd followed her yesterday to apologize, but the truth of it was, watching her march out of his room had forced him to face his feelings. She was the one thing he'd always wanted, but had been afraid to have. He'd been trying to protect himself from the damnable Cavanaugh curse.

Leaving the house by horseback, he went downtown to the East Central Railroad office building and spent the remainder of the day going over contracts that needed to be renewed before the end of the year.

He did that for the next several days, hid in his office, behind paperwork. The contracts did need to be renewed, but they were so standardized, very little needed to be changed.

Therefore, those days had done little more than allow him to think of Harper. For as long as he could remember, he knew what to expect. His life had been mapped out at birth. Even the death of his parents hadn't changed it, nor Kent's untimely passing. He'd still known what was expected of him and what to expect from others.

Until Harper.

It had been a Tuesday. March the second. The first time he'd seen her. That depot had been Kent's territory, but he'd asked for some help with the transfer station, so Kurt had taken the train up there. Then walked into the café and stopped dead in his tracks.

She hadn't rushed to wait on him, like the others, nor had she tried to make him notice her. But he had. He'd gone every day, but it wasn't until the Friday when she'd waited on him, and only then because he'd stayed until there had been an open seat in her area.

He'd asked her recommendation for a meal, and the moment she'd smiled had been the moment he'd lost his heart.

He'd never gotten it back because it belonged to her. Whether she knew it or not.

That was something he was going to have to get used to. She and Katie Jo were a part of his life and always would be. Hiding out at the office wasn't going to change that.

He decided to head home and, upon entering the house, found Katie Jo and Grandpa in the front room, sitting on the floor near the ceiling-height Christmas tree. One of three decorated trees that were in various rooms.

"We're setting up our new train," Katie Jo told him. "We are going to run the track all the way around the tree. Just like at the store."

"New train?" Kurt looked at his grandfather.

"Yes," Grandpa answered. "Get down here and help. This thing is harder to put together than real ones."

The large pile of track pieces looked like work indeed, which was exactly what he needed. Something to focus on. Just like he had when his parents died. He'd wanted to sit down and bawl his eyes out, but he hadn't. Kent had, and because of that, he'd known he had to be the strong one. The one to keep on chugging away, just like this little train would once they got it set up. Grandpa would light the wick in the alcohol-filled miniature firebox, heating up the water in the tiny boiler until it had enough steam to move along the tracks.

That's what he'd done when Kent had died, too, just kept going.

Some things never changed.

All three of them were waiting for the steam to build up and the train to start moving along the completed track, when Harper entered the room. Her dark blue dress enhanced her hourglass shape, and his heart pounded a little harder. She'd been wearing the dresses his grandfather had purchased for the past few days. For some reason, Kurt found a comparison between Harper and himself. She kept on chugging along, too. No matter what.

He knew why they both did that. For their families.

The four of them in this room were all the family any of them had now.

The layers of skirts swished as she walked, and the way she wrinkled her nose said she could smell the alcohol burning on the wick.

He pointed at the train. "We are waiting for the steam to build up."

"It'll go all the way around the Christmas tree," Katie Jo supplied. "See the tracks? Uncle Kurt put them all together. Grandpa built the train and I put up all the buildings and signs, even a bridge."

Grandpa patted the floor. "Join us. It shouldn't be long now."

Kurt stood. "Perhaps we could all move to chairs."

"No," Grandpa said. "It might not work and we'll need to get down here again. These old bones can't move as fast as your young ones."

"Sit here, Harper." Katie Jo patted the floor. "So you can see when it goes over the bridge."

"All right," Harper replied.

Kurt didn't miss the tiny smile she shot his way, nor how it made his heart beat faster. He lowered himself back onto the floor once she was seated between him and Katie Jo. "I was told you were going over lesson plans," he whispered.

"Yes, I was," she whispered.

"And?"

"I'm afraid she will be so far ahead she'll be bored when she returns to the classroom."

"We could end the tutoring sessions," he suggested.

"No, I'm sure Miss Carpenter will be able to accommodate her."

The idea of them leaving didn't sit well. He laid his hand over the top of hers, on the floor between them. "This house is going to be empty when you leave. Very empty."

She let out a long sigh. "She already loves it here so much."

"She loves Pine City, too," he whispered. "She's always going to love anywhere that the two of you are, as long as you are both happy." To reinforce that, he folded his fingers around hers. "If you weren't here, she wouldn't be happy. She'd be missing you too much."

Harper looked at him thoughtfully.

"I'm right," he whispered. "You know I am."

She nodded. "You are. Thank you."

After kissing her as he had, holding her hand should be insignificant, but it wasn't. It was special, and made him wonder if it was time that he took a chance. She'd risked everything by coming here; maybe it was time he did the same.

They sat like that, on the floor, with him holding her hand, while watching the train chug along the track around the tree and over the bridge. Such a simple thing, yet more enjoyable than anyone would probably believe.

The little train slowly rolled to a stop, having run out of steam at the same time that Lincoln entered the room, declaring that dinner was ready.

Grandpa said that was perfect timing, because they needed to let the engine cool down before they could refill the tanks.

Kurt stood, assisted Harper to her feet and kept a hand on her elbow to escort her to the dining room, while Grandpa and Katie Jo hurried ahead, talking about trains and how they needed two engines.

This visit had reinvigorated his grandfather back to the man Kurt had known when he was young. Grandpa had always made sure that he and Kent had fun as children, perhaps because he'd known that would end once they grew up.

Kurt stopped in the arched doorway, bringing Harper to a stop beside him. "I just want to say thank you. Thank you for coming here. I haven't seen my grandfather this happy in years. If ever. Most people only ever saw him as a hard man, a businessman, but he wasn't that way with me and Kent. Not when we were young. He had his moments after we'd grown up, but—" He shook his head. "After Kent died, he slowed down, then turned everything over to me and just holed himself up here, in the house. The doctor said it was age, and I accepted that, but now I think it was because he didn't have anything to live for. He does now, because of you. Thank you."

Harper couldn't tell him everything that was in her heart. She wasn't sure she knew herself. It was all too complicated. Even though he'd been home in the evenings the past few days, she'd sensed a distance in him. It wasn't there tonight, and she knew what he'd just said had come from his heart. "You're welcome," she said, "but I also need to thank you. Katie Jo is happier than I've ever seen her. She's thoroughly enjoying doing things, seeing things that she'd never get to experience in Pine City. Not to mention the people here. I was wrong to keep her from her family. From you and her grandfather."

"You are her family, too."

"I am, but I wasn't very good at sharing her." Harper had come to another conclusion over the past few days. She and Katie Jo were living the life that Sherri had dreamed about having, and Harper knew that Sherri would be happy to know that Katie Jo was here, in her father's house. Even as sick and sad as Sherri had been, she'd kept insisting that her child would have a wonderful life. Harper had agreed and had vowed to see that happen. "I should have been. She's so happy."

"What about you? Are you happy?"

That's where things got complicated. Seeing Katie Jo happy made her happy. He had made her happy, too. Many times by things he'd done, but also by the person he was. He was a good man, a caring man. She couldn't expect anything more. "Yes, I'm happy."

"Good."

They stood there, looking at each other. Harper couldn't read his mind, probably because hers was too busy remembering when they'd kissed. That moment would live inside her for eternity.

Something above him fell, landed on his head.

"What the—" He reached up, plucked it off his head and held it between them.

A sprig of mistletoe. It was hanging from nearly every doorway and chandelier, and a small leaf of it was in Katie Jo's hope chest, among a treasure trove of other things she'd collected since arriving. Harper wasn't saving mementos, but would forever cherish a few memories.

"The tack came loose," he said, turning the stem

so she could see the little metal tack that had been holding the sprig in the doorway above them.

"It must have," she said, barely breathing, because she was wondering if she dared.

He looked at the mistletoe, then at her again.

Her heart somersaulted, then something else happened. A boldness she'd never witnessed in herself rose up, and she stretched onto her toes.

The next moment, she was once again glorying in the feel of his lips against hers. Looking at him years ago had made her melt, but she never imagined that kissing him would liquefy every part of her. That's what it did. Put her in a floating, dreamlike state of being.

It wasn't a long kiss like the one in his suite. It was short and precious in a way that left her sighing when their lips parted.

She met his eyes and smiled. It was impossible not to. He was smiling, too.

Chapter Eleven

"Would you care to take a carriage ride with me?" Kurt asked her on Saturday morning, after breakfast.

She probably should have contemplated her answer, but didn't want to. Since their second kiss under the mistletoe, she truly had found a deep and profound happiness in the unique companionship that had formed between them. "Yes."

Moments later, bundled in her coat and walking toward the carriage, she asked, "Where are we going?"

"Nowhere in particular," he said. "It's a nice day, I thought you might like to get outside, perhaps see some of the city. We can go shopping if you'd like."

"I went yesterday with Katie Jo and Grandpa."

Once settled on the seat, sharing a lap blanket, he asked, "Did they buy another train?"

She shot him a sideways glance. "They couldn't buy just an engine."

He laughed. "Well, at least I didn't get stuck putting the track together."

Patting his knee, she said, "Don't count your blessings too soon. They are being delivered today."

"They?"

She shrugged. "There are three Christmas trees in the house."

He laughed and laid a hand atop the one she still had on his knee. "Sit back and enjoy the ride as I point out some of Baltimore's finest attributes, because we'll be busy laying track when we get back home."

"We?"

He grinned while nodding. "Yes, we."

They traveled up and down streets, past various businesses housed in brick and wooden buildings, tree-filled parks and neighborhoods full of lovely homes, over bridges and past historical sites, and so many other places, she'd never be able to remember everything. Then the carriage came to a stop next to an immense brick building. It was eleven stories high, with arched brickwork surrounding the windows on the ground floor that were as tall as the door, which was also massive and made of glass. The doorway was uniquely positioned right on the corner of two streets, giving the building two fronts. It was very impressive.

"What is this?" she asked.

He folded back the blanket, then flipped down the step on the side of the carriage and climbed out.

She took his hand and stepped down onto the concrete sidewalk, still waiting for his answer. He'd readily offered information, including unique details about so many other places, so she was excited to know about this one. "Is it a hotel?" she asked, taking a guess.

"No." He took her hand and led her between the two large stone columns that held up the arched roof of the building's forecourt. It was then that she saw the name carved in the granite stone above the door. East Central Railroad.

"This is your building?" she asked.

"Yes."

A man wearing a blue uniform, with gold ropes on the shoulders, opened one of the glass doors and held it for them to enter.

"Good day, Mr. Cavanaugh."

"Good day to you, Douglas," Kurt replied. "This is Miss Hollister."

"Miss, it's my pleasure."

"Thank you," she replied, stepping inside. Made of white and gray marble, the lobby was gorgeous, with sweeping staircases on both sides, and on the back wall, carved in the marble, was a huge locomotive.

Harper didn't know if she should be breathless, or scared. Or both. She'd known the East Central Railroad was the first railroad in the nation, but she truly hadn't understood the significance of that, or of the Cavanaugh family, until this moment.

"Will you be going up, sir?" the man asked.

"Yes, Douglas," Kurt answered.

He led her to a door that turned out to be an elevator, and Douglas operated the levers, taking them upward. She watched a dial above the door click from number to number, all the way to the last one. Eleven.

"We won't be long, Douglas," Kurt said as the man opened the door.

"I'll be here, sir."

Kurt opened a door across the hall, and she entered. It was an office, with a large carved desk, chairs and filing cabinets, maps and pictures of trains on the walls.

"This is your office?" she asked.

"No. This is my secretary's office. Mine is through here."

He opened another door. She walked past him, into the room. The first office had been nice, very nice, but this one was unbelievable. A huge desk was in the center, and there was a variety of other furniture. Bookcases, filing cabinets, chairs, tables, even a sofa. More maps and train pictures on the walls. But it was the windows that drew her attention. Behind the desk, the glass went from nearly the floor to the ceiling, and the view was indescribable. It looked out over the city. Buildings that had looked large from the ground, looked small from up here. So did the park, and the trams and carriages on the streets looked nearly as small as the toy train beneath the tree at the house.

"I've never been this high up in my life," she said. "It's amazing."

Kurt stepped up beside her. "The building was finished three years ago. Kent helped design it, back in its infancy. He drew the train that is carved in the wall downstairs."

"It's beautiful. All of it. Including the carving." Twisting, she looked at him. "Did you grow up wanting to work for the railroad?"

"I grew up knowing I'd work at the railroad," he replied. "I was seven, Kent was six when our parents died. They were ferrying across the bay, and the ferry went down. Grandpa said that it didn't change anything, I imagine in an attempt to help us move on. But he was right. It didn't. I'm in the exact same place I would have been if they hadn't died."

Harper let a sigh slowly escape. Oddly enough, her father had said the same thing when her mother died. Nothing in their lives was really different, other than missing her mother tremendously. It hadn't been until

Sherri died that her life had been completely changed. Pulling up a smile, she gestured at the room. "Well, I wouldn't call this nowhere in particular."

Kurt chuckled at the reference to his earlier comment. "I hadn't planned on bringing you here when we left the house. I decided as we drove around, because I want you to know what's behind you. What's supporting you. Because all of this, all that I own, all that my grandfather owns, is here for you."

"You mean it's here for Katie Jo."

"It is here for Katie Jo, but also for you." He'd never been more aware of another person in so many ways. She had the ability to make him go tongue-tied, to make his mind blank and his palms sweat. His heart beat faster. He'd wanted her to see all of this, not to impress her, but to show her the resources that he wanted to share with her. The life he wanted to share with her. It was a risk, because she could say no. She could also say yes.

She straightened slightly as she met his gaze with a direct stare.

He was the owner of the oldest and largest train company in the nation, yet, at times, felt like a schoolboy around her. "I like you, Harper."

"I—I like you, too, Kurt."

He wasn't asking for a confession, but liked hearing her say that, even though she sounded wary.

"I like how it feels as if we can read each other's minds at times. Like when we interviewed for the tutor, or when Katie Jo or Grandpa say or do something."

"I like that, too," she said, sounding more comfortable. "It's made things easier at times."

"It has." A single point became crystal clear in his mind. A curse was only a curse if a man let it be one. He wasn't going to let it. "I don't know who broke your heart, Harper, or when—"

"I did," she said, "by putting expectations on someone who knew nothing about them. But it turned out well. I discovered that I didn't need to be rescued."

He took hold of her hands. "I would have rescued you, had I known."

She met his gaze. "I know you would have."

Kurt couldn't tell her the truth. Not the truth in his heart. The one that included all the desires, wants and dreams he had about her. It would scare her. She'd be on the next northbound train in the flash of an eye, which was the last thing he wanted. But he could still tell her another truth. "I remember the first time I saw you. It was a Tuesday, but you didn't wait on me until the end of the week."

"Because everyone knew who you were and rushed to wait on you."

"Did you know who I was?"

"Yes." She grinned. "How could I not? The moment you walked in, whispers started."

"You acted like I was an average customer."

"You weren't average."

"Neither were you. I've never known anyone so caring, giving and kind."

She let out a long sigh. "I wasn't very kind. I listened to things that were said about your family, believed things that I shouldn't have. I never said anything bad in front of Katie Jo. Then again, that's because I lied to her, said I was her sister instead of her aunt. That was not kind, either. It wasn't fair to think so poorly about Kent, or treat Sherri as I did. I kept telling her to get up, that she was going to lie in that bed and die."

Kurt wrapped his arms around her as tears trickled from her eyes. "There now, you can't blame yourself for that."

"Yes, I can," she said with a sob. "She was convinced Kent loved her and was sad about his marriage, but she'd been sick from the time she became pregnant. Nothing would stay down. The doctor who delivered Katie said it's that way sometimes. That often neither mother or baby live, and there's nothing that could have been done. But I should have done *something*. More than telling her to get up."

Kurt kissed the top of her head. "You did do something. You took care of her when she had no one else. Then you took care of Katie Jo. All by yourself." He hugged her tighter. Kissed her hair. "We can't change the past."

"I know," she said.

He leaned back and lifted her face. "But we can change the future." Then, even though there was no mistletoe overhead, he kissed her. The way she returned that kiss gave him hope. Enough hope to fill a hope chest.

Chapter Twelve

In the days that followed, Kurt had a new lease on life. He wanted to be with Harper, as much as possible, and assigned duties at work that he normally handled personally, to give himself more free time. Trusted employees had been the foundation that had allowed the company to grow and succeed. He'd known that, but in the past, he'd only assigned his duties to others when he'd needed to be gone for other business. Doing so for personal reasons would have felt as if he was shirking his duties.

It didn't feel that way now, because he didn't let it.

There was other business he needed to see to, and it didn't have anything to do with the railroad. He had made a decision. Cavanaugh curse be damned.

"I'll have these drawn up today," Neil said.

"Send them to the house," Kurt said. "Not the office."

"All right." Neil took off his glasses and leaned

back in his chair, folded his arms. "I'm gone for ten days and come home to one of my best friends getting married and adopting a child."

Kurt couldn't hide the happiness inside him, nor did he try. He'd explained everything to Neil, about Kent and Sherri, Katie Jo and Harper. "Some things just work out."

"Good for you. I expect to be invited to the wedding."

Kurt had yet to ask Harper, but was growing more confident each day that she would say yes. They'd become closer the past week, and neither of them missed an opportunity to steal a kiss beneath one of the many sprigs of mistletoe hanging in the house. "You will be," he replied while standing and held out a hand. "Thanks, Neil."

Neil stood, and they shook hands. "I'll have the papers delivered to your house tomorrow morning."

Kurt left the lawyer's office and instructed Tony to drive to his next stop. The jewelry store. There were three days left until Christmas, and he had a plan in place. He would give Harper the ring on Christmas Eve and the adoption papers on Christmas morning. Spread out the joy.

Harper twisted left, then right, examining her reflection in the mirror, looking for any pine needles.

The dress was very stylish, silver blue, with a fitted waist and a wide row of lace sewn vertically from the collar to the waist. It fit her perfectly.

"I've been thinking, Harper," Katie Jo said from where she sat on the bed in Harper's room, with Paws sitting beside her.

"About what?"

"Paws."

Harper walked to the bed and stroked the dog's soft fur. "What about him?"

"I didn't get him a Christmas present. When I went shopping with Grandpa yesterday, I got one for everyone else, but not Paws."

Harper held out a hand. "You have time. There are still three days until Christmas. Come now, neither of us have any pine sap left on us, and Uncle Kurt should be home by now."

Katie Jo grabbed her hand, leaped off the bed and shot out the door, with Paws running beside her. "Yippie! I can't wait for him to see the lights!"

Harper pressed a hand to her stomach before walking to the door. Three days until Christmas. She felt like she was watching an hourglass, dropping grains of sand from one glass bulb to the other. There had been times during the past few days when her feelings had been so intense for Kurt, she'd almost asked him if he'd mind if they stayed longer.

She was sure that he'd say yes.

The problem was, staying wouldn't solve anything.

They hadn't discussed exactly when she and Katie Jo would return to Pine City, nor when Katie Jo would return for another visit. That would happen, Harper had no doubt about that. But this was the only time she would accompany Katie Jo for visits here. Katie Jo didn't need her here. She had her uncle and great-grandfather. Harper would miss her niece greatly during those times. She would miss Kurt and Axel, too, but would never again put expectations where they didn't belong. That had only led to heartache, and she wouldn't do that to herself again.

Until then…

Kurt was standing at the bottom of the steps as she arrived at the top of the stairway, and her heart doubled in size.

Until then, she'd be the happiest woman in the world. "Hello. How was your day?"

"From the sounds of it, not as exciting as yours," he answered.

Axel had heard about electric lights for Christmas trees and had ordered several strands from a company in New York. "Yes, the lights arrived today." She reached the bottom step and sighed silently at the touch of his hand on her arm.

"Enough for all of the trees?"

"All three of them. By the time the two of them got them on all three trees, Katie Jo was covered in pine pitch, and so was Axel."

"And you?"

She shrugged. "They needed help."

He laughed, then lifted her chin and gave her a thorough kiss.

Even her toes were tingling when their lips parted. "What did you do today?"

"Signed more contracts than I could count for next year, visited with my lawyer and then I went shopping."

"Shopping? Are you taking after your grandfather?"

He smiled. "I only bought one thing."

They entered the front room, and moments later, the tree was lit up. It looked magical with all of the lights, but they quickly grew warm and needed to be turned off.

The lights were turned on again after the evening meal and one last time before it was time for Katie Jo to go to bed. As normal, Axel retired to his room, too, and after tucking Katie Jo into her bed, Harper met Kurt in the library.

Her stomach fluttered as she walked into the room, just as it had done each night prior.

He met her near the door. "This is my favorite time of day."

"Mine, too," she whispered as their lips met.

They stayed in the library until late, holding hands, talking and kissing. Harper knew she was letting herself fall deeply in love with him. Too deeply, but that was something she couldn't control.

Later than night, while alone in her bed, she fully understood that she couldn't stay beyond Christmas. Her womanly desires were getting too hard to fight, and if she didn't leave soon, she could end up just like Sherri.

Unwed and pregnant.

When Kurt left for work the following morning, he said he'd be home before the noon meal and, because it was snowing, promised Katie Jo that they would go tobogganing.

Mrs. Gallagher arrived on time as always, but less than an hour later, Lincoln came into the front room where Harper and Axel were playing a game of cards.

"Excuse me, miss, sir," Lincoln said. "The snow is piling up, and it might be safer if the tutor was given a ride home before the bridge becomes impassable."

Axel looked at her, and Harper nodded. The moisture coming off the bay caused the bridge to become ice coated, and snow made it worse. Horses could easily lose their footing. "Of course. Right away. I'll go let her know."

Moments later, Mrs. Gallagher was ready to leave, and as Lincoln opened the door, a young messenger was trudging up the snow-covered walkway.

"I have a delivery for Mr. Kurt Cavanaugh," the young man said, wiping snow off the envelope. "I'm sorry. I tripped and it fell in the snow."

"Thank you," Lincoln said, taking the wet envelope.

The young man turned to leave, and Harper stepped forward. "Are you walking?"

"Yes, ma'am. My horse refused to cross the bridge. It's not that bad, yet. He just doesn't like bridges. I tied him up on the other side."

Harper stepped onto the porch and gestured for Tony to wait, then told the young man, "Our driver will give you a ride to your horse."

"Thank you, ma'am," he said. "Thank you very much."

The young man ran to the carriage, and Harper stepped back inside the house, where Katie Jo was looking at her expectantly. Her spelling test had been interrupted, and Harper had assured her that she would finish giving her the words.

She held out her hand and the two of them walked towards the library.

"I'm an exceptional speller," Katie Jo told Lincoln, who was also walking to the library.

"I am aware of that, miss," he replied with a smile and a wink. "I'm just going to lay this letter out to dry on the desk and then be out of your way."

While Lincoln went to the desk, Harper and Katie Jo settled at the table, and Harper began the test where Mrs. Gallagher had indicated.

Four words later, Katie Jo broke the lead on her pencil. "I'll get another one," she said, knowing where they were in the holder on the desk.

Harper waited at the table. When Katie Jo remained at the desk too long, she asked, "What are you doing?"

"What's an ado—adoptee?"

Not understanding at all, Harper stood and walked to the desk. The words on the single wet sheet of paper made her heart fall all the way to her toes.

"What is it?" Katie Jo pointed at the paper. "That's my name. It says Katherine. That's me."

It did say Katherine. As the adoptee on a legal document. And the adopter was none other than Mr. Kurt Cavanaugh.

Harper couldn't breathe. It felt as if she'd taken a blow straight to the chest so hard the wind had been knocked out of her.

"What is it, Harper?"

"Nothing. Just a letter. Come, let's go upstairs."

"But my spelling test."

"We'll finish it later." Harper had no idea what she was going to do, other than not stay here. Not give him the chance to do the one thing he'd promised not to do. He'd been lying to her the entire time. Making her fall in love with him so... Why? So that she wouldn't object?

She objected all right.

Grabbing the piece of paper, she tugged Katie Jo upstairs.

Katie Jo was full of questions, but also minded well enough that both of them were soon dressed in their own clothes, the ones they'd arrived in. Knowing she couldn't carry all of their belongings, Harper put only a few additional articles of clothing and Katie Jo's hope chest into her small suitcase.

Not wanting to have Katie Jo overly upset, she said they were going shopping and, even though it was snowing, they would be fine.

They would be. It wasn't that far. Only a few blocks after the bridge was a tram that they could take to the train station.

Chapter Thirteen

Kurt arrived to a house that was in full chaos. Paws was barking, his grandfather shouting and people running about.

"What's happening?" Kurt asked. "Where's Harper?"

"You did this!" Grandpa shouted, wagging a finger at him. "You! Not me!"

"I didn't do anything," Kurt said, and noting his grandfather's coat, asked, "Where are you going?"

"By God, man! Where do you think? To look for them!"

"For who?" he shouted in return. Then he shouted at Paws "Be quiet!"

The dog ran to the door and scratched at it frantically.

His level of concern skyrocketed and, heart pounding, he asked, "Where are Harper and Katie Jo?"

"I don't know! Paws was shut in Katie Jo's room, barking his head off! We've looked everywhere—they aren't here! They're gone!"

"Gone?" The pounding of his heart was echoing in his head, and for the life of him, he couldn't figure out why Harper would have left.

"Tony's not back yet. Abner's bringing around the other carriage. I'm going to find them," Grandpa said. "You're going to fix this!"

Kurt didn't reply, just shot out the door. There was only one place they would go. Due to the weather, he'd ridden horseback this morning and ran to the horse tethered to the post. He hadn't seen anything along the road, but Harper would know that it would be much shorter to walk along the shoreline to the bridge.

Sure enough, there were footprints in the snow. The huge flakes that had fallen for most of the morning had eased, but it was cold, and he couldn't imagine Harper taking Katie Jo out in such conditions without a very good reason.

Not knowing what that reason could be was eating him alive.

Due to traffic on the road, the footprints ended after climbing up the hill by the bridge, but he was certain he knew where he'd find them.

Arriving at the train station, he left his horse near the door and ran inside. The depot wasn't overly busy, and he instantly saw her standing at the ticket booth. Katie Jo was standing beside her, and while tentatively waving at him with one hand, she pulled on Harper's coat sleeve with the other.

Harper turned, and the anger in her eyes reminded him of when she'd first realized he was in Pine City.

She was safe, and unhurt—physically. Gaining an ounce of control, he walked to the ticket booth. Money was lying on the counter, and he covered it with his hand. "She doesn't need any tickets."

Her glare was filled with defiance. "Yes, I do."

"If you need to travel anywhere, we'll take the Pullman car."

Her eyes narrowed as they stared at one another.

The ticket attendant, clearly not knowing what to do, asked, "Would you like me to have your private car prepared for travel, Mr. Cavanaugh?"

Now that he'd found them, Kurt was no longer filled with fear, nor was he mad. He was merely confused, so waited for her to respond.

Barking broke the silence surrounding them. He wasn't surprised that his grandfather had brought Paws with him, nor that he'd been followed. "Katie Jo, Grandpa's outside in the carriage."

Katie Jo looked at Harper, and he did, too, with a challenge for her to defy him.

She was clearly mad, but gave Katie Jo a nod.

He watched as Katie Jo ran to the door where

Abner stood, then he turned to the ticket attendant. "I'll let you know momentarily."

With a firm hold, he moved Harper away from the booth. "Tell me what is going on here."

"You lied," she said. "This whole time you've been lying."

"About what?"

She shook her head. "As if you don't know."

"I don't."

The daggers in her eyes would have killed him if they were bullets, but the only thing that hit him was a balled-up piece of paper.

It bounced off his chest before he caught it. He smoothed it out with both hands. The paper looked as if it had been wet, the ink slightly smeared, but he recognized it. "This is why you're so mad?"

"Yes! You had adoption papers drawn up! For you to adopt her!"

He looked at the single piece of paper and a chill rippled up his spine. "Where's the rest of this?"

She didn't reply.

"The envelope this came in, where is it? This is only the first page."

The color was slipping from her face, and the idea that she trusted him so little made his stomach sink.

The ride back to the house, with both of them on

his horse, and her holding on to the small suitcase, was cold and quiet.

Once there, he led her into the library and closed the door. This was why he'd protected his heart. It ached, knowing he'd hurt her. Ached knowing she thought he'd been lying to her. Just ached.

He picked the envelope up off the desk and pulled out several other sheets of paper. Flipping through them, he found the second set of adoption papers. "Here."

She took the paper and a tear fell from the corner of one eye.

"As you can see," Kurt said, "it's a second set of adoption papers. Your papers to adopt Katie Jo, so you can legally be her mother. Forever."

"I'm sorry," she whispered. "So sorry. The first page got wet, so it was the only one I saw and I…" She lifted her gaze to him. "Why was there that first page?"

"Because I legally want to be her father," he said. "I was hoping that you would want that, too. For us to be her parents."

She stared at him for the longest minute of his life, then took several steps backward, shaking her head. "That can't happen."

"Yes, it can." He dug in his coat pocket, pulled out the ring he'd picked up from the jeweler that morning. "I was going to give this to you on Christmas Eve, ask you to marry—"

"No! You can't." She flattened a hand over her forehead. "I can't."

"Why?"

She set the papers on the desk. "Katie Jo—"

"I'm not asking you to marry me because of Katie Jo. I'm asking you because of who *you* are," he admitted. "I was afraid of the way you made me feel from the first time I saw you. In you, I saw something that wasn't predetermined, something that I would have to earn. I knew how to buy things, build things, but I'd never had to earn anything. I didn't have a clue as to how to do that and made mistakes along the way. Including those adoption papers. I should have told you about them, but I was waiting to show you. Show you that she's yours forever. I wanted to earn your love more than I'd ever wanted anything."

She was still shaking her head, now with her hand over her mouth.

"I love you, Harper. I love everything about you. Your loyalty, your compassion, your devotion and even your stubbornness." He took a step toward her. "I refuse to believe that you don't love me in return."

Tears trickled from her eyes. "I do love you," she whispered. "Have loved you for a long time, but

I couldn't expect..." She covered her mouth with one hand.

His heart no longer ached. It was overflowing. "Expect me to love you? You should have, because I have loved you since March second, almost seven years ago. The moment I saw you. I never thought love at first sight was a real thing, but I now know it very much is."

Harper's heart was swelling inside her chest, becoming so large she could feel it thumping against her rib cage. "I know it's real, too," she whispered.

Kurt stared at her for a moment, then lifted her hand and slowly slid the ring, which held not one, but two large diamonds surrounded by several smaller ones, onto her finger. "You can expect my love. You can expect much more than that. You can expect me to provide for you, for Katie Jo. You can expect me to always think of you first, before the railroad, before anyone or anything. And you can expect me to be right here, waiting for you, when you decide if you want to marry me."

"There is no *if,*" she whispered. "I do want to marry you. I'm just afraid."

"Of what?"

"Of doing just what I did. Of disappointing you."

He cupped her face with both hands. "I'm not asking you to be perfect, although you are as close as anyone can be. I'm asking you to love me, to marry me, so we can face whatever life brings us together."

She could do that. All of that. She already loved him, had for years, and would never, ever question his intentions or love for her again.

Harper wrapped her arms around Kurt's waist and held on tight as he hugged her, wondering how she had ever imagined that she could live her life without him. She'd tried that once and it hadn't worked out well. "I'm sorry. Sorry for thinking the worst of you. I will never do that again. I should have known better, but I was so afraid of loving you again. The top letter was the only one on the desk. I never considered looking in the envelope. Not that I ever read other people's mail. Lincoln had laid it out to dry and Katie Jo saw her name on it. Asked what it was."

He leaned back, frowning. "Afraid of loving me *again*?"

"Yes, it was love at first sight for me, too, but after Katie Jo was born, I was so afraid of losing her that I had to tell myself that I didn't love you. That I couldn't love both her and you."

His frown deepened. "Is that what you meant about having your heart broken?"

"Yes." Not wanting him to feel any blame, she

quickly added, "It was all my fault, and now I know that I can love both of you, and I do, so very much."

"I love you, too." He glanced at the desk. "And I promise that I will never try to surprise you again."

She stretched on her toes, so their mouths almost touched. "I don't mind surprises. I don't mind being rescued, either."

"Rescued?"

She nodded. "From doing silly things like buying train tickets."

He laughed, kissed her until her toes curled in her boots. "Anytime you and Katie Jo need to visit Pine City, a Pullman car will be at your service." Looking deep into her eyes, he asked, "Harper Hollister, will you please marry me?"

This was it, her dream coming true. "Yes, Kurt Cavanaugh, I will marry you." She'd never wanted to be a blue blood, but that certainly wasn't going to stop her from loving him. Nothing would ever stop her from loving him, or from spending the rest of her life as his wife. Stretching on her toes, she kissed him with all the urgency and love that she'd kept bottled up for so long.

Releasing it made her so happy. So very happy.

They were both breathing hard and laughing when their lips parted.

He glanced at the door. "I suppose we should go let the others know that everything is all right."

Harper looked up, not surprised to see that they were standing beneath the chandelier, and a sprig of mistletoe. "I suppose we should, but we could wait just a little longer."

"We'll tell them later." His lips touched hers as he added, "Much later."

Being a Cavanaugh had advantages, and Kurt proved that to her in several ways, including arranging for them to be wed after midnight mass on Christmas Eve.

Many in the congregation stayed to witness the event. That didn't bother Harper—she was too happy to care about anything except the man she was marrying.

Once she became Mrs. Kurt Cavanaugh, they rode home in the carriage with Axel and Katie Jo, who were both overjoyed by the union.

"Look, Grandpa," Katie Jo said, pointing at the sky. "A falling star."

"No, darling," Axel said. "That's old Saint Nick in his miniature sleigh being pulled by eight tiny reindeer."

"It is?" Katie Jo asked.

Harper looked at Kurt, and shared one of their mind reading moments.

"You can still make a wish," Kurt said to Katie Jo.

"I don't need to," she answered. "My greatest hope came true."

"What was that?" Harper asked.

"A family. That's what I've been hoping for, for a long time."

"You have that, darling," Axel said. "Always will."

Harper leaned her head on Kurt's shoulder. That had been the hope she'd had in her heart for years, too. And he'd made it happen.

Epilogue

Before the last train whistle faded, another one sounded again, and again. Harper knew why. She looked at Kurt, who was smiling as brightly as Axel, sitting across from them on the padded passenger seats.

"That girl blows a good whistle," Axel said with pride.

Harper was sure that Axel would have liked to have ridden the last twenty miles in the engine room, too, but because Mr. Duncan, who had given up the stage-coach to engineer the train, was still an apprentice, there wasn't enough room.

Though Katie Jo loved her life in Baltimore, whenever she mentioned missing Pine City, Kurt took them on a trip to see everyone. And when Katie Jo said that it would be nice if a train went all the way there, he'd had tracks built. He claimed that it was a good business investment, that the area needed a way to transport goods, as well as people. Harper believed him, but she also knew that he'd do anything for their daughter.

"She's been waiting for this day for a year and half," Kurt said. "That's a long time to a child." He laid a hand on Harper's stomach. "Nine months is a long time for parents to wait, too."

Overflowing with happiness, Harper covered his hands with both of hers. "We only have three more months to wait."

"I still think it's going to be a boy," Axel said. "Have I mentioned what a nice name Axel is?"

"Several times," Kurt replied.

"Remember that," Axel said.

The whistle blew again as the train rolled to a stop and band music could be heard inside the passenger car. Harper looked at Kurt, sharing a look that said the entire town was outside.

"Did you expect anything less?" she asked, laughing.

"No," he said. "Katie Jo's arrival has been an anticipated event."

Although the train had its own legal call number, the shiny black engine had the name Katie Jo painted in white on both sides.

The changes that had happened since she'd married him were not just for herself and Katie Jo. The entire town of Pine City was benefiting, and none of that was lost on her.

Kurt took hold of her hand and helped her stand. She looped her arms around his neck and brought her lips close to his. "I love you."

"I love seeing you happy," he whispered, then kissed her, proving it.

She already knew that, but didn't mind the reminder.

* * * * *

COMING SOON!

We really hope you enjoyed reading this book. If you're looking for more romance be sure to head to the shops when new books are available on

Thursday 23rd November

To see which titles are coming soon, please visit
millsandboon.co.uk/nextmonth

MILLS & BOON

MILLS & BOON ®

Coming next month

MISS ROSE AND THE VEXING VISCOUNT
Catherine Tinley

'You really ought not to be falling asleep with a candle alight, Miss Lennox. Particularly—' he gestured at the floor-to-ceiling bookshelves '—in a library.'

Rubbing a hand over her face, she shook her head. There was a silence, as James found himself rooted to the spot. She, adorably bemused. He, hoping his own bewilderment was not evident in his expression.

Lord, she is like a goddess!

Their eyes met, and instantly the atmosphere was charged with possibility—as tense as the air before a thunderstorm. The urge to kiss her was almost overwhelming... There was puzzlement in her gaze, as well as—Lord save him—desire. She desired him!

But no. She had likely never even been kissed, and might have no notion what she was feeling. Focusing on her clear confusion, he reminded himself sternly that she was his aunt's guest, and he the master of the house.

I am a viscount, not some green boy free to dally with a chambermaid.

And she was no courtesan or merry widow, but a young lady of quality.

Breaking her gaze, he brushed an imaginary speck from his right sleeve, then pretended to stifle a yawn.

'It is late. I was surprised to see a light in here.'

Hearing her exhale in something like relief, he was conscious of a strong feeling of disappointment.

'Yes, of course. I apologise, my lord.'

He nodded, then briefly, daringly, he allowed his gaze to sweep once more over her form, delightfully hinted at through the thin fabric. As he watched, transfixed, she tied the belt on her sheer peignoir—a garment trimmed, he noted, in rosebud pink.

'I could not sleep, you see,' she continued, 'and so I came downstairs to choose a book…' Confusion briefly flashed across her face and she looked about, bending to pick the book up from the floor.

'Oh, dear! I do hope I have not damaged it!'

Rising, she inspected the small tome, turning towards the candle on the table to see better. Unfortunately, this gave him an unhindered view of her delectable rear, glorious golden curls cascading down her back, her shapely legs outlined through two layers of thin, candlelit fabric. Stifling a groan, he turned away. 'I shall bid you goodnight, Miss Lennox,' he threw the comment over his shoulder as he made for the door. 'Do try not to burn my house down, I beseech you.'

On that note he left the room, marching briskly to the staircase that would take him to the sanctuary of his own chamber. Lord, he had expected his quiet life to be disturbed by his aunt's debutantes. Just—never had he expected the disturbance to be quite so…personal.

Continue reading
MISS ROSE AND THE VEXING VISCOUNT
Catherine Tinley

Available next month
www.millsandboon.co.uk